"How can you sell people rubbish like this?"

The painting in Robert Beaumont's hands was revealed in the glare of the studio lights as the amateurish work it really was.

"I liked it," Kate lied. She could hardly say she'd exhibited it out of pity for the old man who'd painted it. "And what's more, I'm willing to bet someone else will like it, too, enough to buy it. We'll refund your money for the picture and rehang it in our gallery, and I'll bet it will be sold within six weeks."

Robert stared at the suspicious brightness of her eyes. "All right, Miss Bowman. I'll take your bet. And if it isn't sold by then, you will come and work for me and try to learn a little about art!"

WELCOME
TO THE WONDERFUL WORLD
OF *Harlequin Romances*

Interesting, informative and entertaining,
each Harlequin Romance portrays an appealing
and original love story. With a varied array
of settings, we may lure you on an African safari,
to a quaint Welsh village, or an exotic Riviera
location—anywhere and everywhere that adventurous
men and women fall in love.

As publishers of Harlequin Romances, we're
extremely proud of our books. Since 1949,
Harlequin Enterprises has built its publishing
reputation on the solid base of quality and
originality. Our stories are the most popular
paperback romances sold in North America; every
month, six new titles are released and sold at
nearly every book-selling store in Canada and the
United States.

For a list of all titles currently available,
send your name and address to:

HARLEQUIN READER SERVICE,
(In the U.S.) P.O. Box 52040, Phoenix, AZ 85072-2040
(In Canada) P.O. Box 2800, Postal Station A
5170 Yonge Street, Willowdale, Ont. M2N 5T5

We sincerely hope you enjoy reading
this Harlequin Romance.

Yours truly,

THE PUBLISHERS
Harlequin Romances

A Place of Wild Honey

Ann Charlton

Harlequin Books

TORONTO • NEW YORK • LONDON
AMSTERDAM • PARIS • SYDNEY • HAMBURG
STOCKHOLM • ATHENS • TOKYO • MILAN

Original hardcover edition published in 1984
by Mills & Boon Limited

ISBN 0-373-02660-9

Harlequin Romance first edition December 1984

For Alan

Printed in U.S.A.

CHAPTER ONE

THE television studio was set high on Mount Coot-tha with the sprawling city and suburbs of Brisbane spread out below it. It was a sight to rival anything that the TV channel beamed out to its two million viewers. Ranks of mountain ash and eucalypts framed rivers, ridges and rooftops in their narrow gaps. Park greens and quarry browns, misty Moreton Bay blues, and everywhere winter sunlight glinting gold.

Not that Kate Bowman saw any of it. By the time her van had negotiated the last curving stretch of the road, her hands were shaking on the wheel. It was no easy thing, she reflected, as she parked near the Channel's massive transmission tower, to appear live on television for the first time.

Beside the car she fiddled with the strap of her bag, putting off the moment when she would walk inside the studio. Magpies made their music high in the trees that ringed the building and a light breeze teased the leaves into dry, rustling accompaniment. 'Coot-tha', the aboriginals had named the mountain—'place of wild honey'. It had changed since others had discovered its beauties and its uses, but still the mountain had its havens. So much peace out here—but in there . . . Kate took a deep breath and wished she'd never written that letter to the newspaper. Wished she'd never heard of Robert Beaumont.

Robert Beaumont.

Kate found the name enough to bring her head up, to quell the worst of her trembling. Green eyes bright with determination, she made her way from the car park through the landscaped rock gardens to the studio entrance.

This was an opportunity to show the pompous art critic that not everyone bowed to his opinions. And heaven knows he had made those opinions very clear. Kate paused by the glass foyer doors, putting up a hand to tuck away a strand of copper hair that had drifted from the knot at the back of her head. She smoothed the collar of her ice green suit and smiled faintly. 'You look marvellous,' her aunt had said before she left. 'Robert Beaumont will probably carry you off instead of arguing with you over your lack of art expertise.'

'No, I can't see him doing that somehow, Louise,' she had laughed. 'I see our unfriendly neighbour as rather less than athletic.'

Kate pushed the doors open, thinking of the effete, overweight critic whose élite gallery was so near to their own struggling one. Of course, she admitted to herself, she didn't *know* that he was overweight or effete—she'd never set eyes on the man, but the image went with the pompous pronouncements he'd made on their gallery. Pale hands, she mused ... and a polo-necked sweater. He'd probably wear one of those. Yes, she could imagine him with pudgy, pale hands clasped over the suggestion of a paunch. Kate was feeling better by the minute.

'Mr Lewis?' the receptionist repeated when she asked for the floor manager of the Backchat show. 'Down the corridor and turn left. He should be somewhere past the film department, or in Studio One.'

But Kate found no trace of Mr Lewis. She looked into several rooms and cursorily into a fourth, intending to go next to the studio.

'Looking for me?'

Kate walked inside the mirrored room to see a man half standing, half sitting against a bench that ran along two walls. Outside someone walked by, heels clacking on the polished floor, but there was absolute silence in here. She looked at the man and felt the silence inside her and an odd warmth growing. Smiling grey eyes met hers and her own smile was instant and genuine.

'Not unless you're Mr Lewis.' She knew he couldn't be. He seemed too at ease to be the floor manager of a show due to start within half an hour.

The man straightened, pushing aside the edges of his blazer to sink his hands in his pockets. 'No, I'm sorry to say I'm not.' His eyes crinkled at the corners as his smile widened. 'Lucky Mr Lewis to have you in pursuit!' There was a disturbing warmth in his eyes, a frankness in his appraisal that would normally threaten Kate's reserve. This was not a man to flirt with. He had the look of one who got what he wanted. Common sense told her not to stand there trading words with this attractive stranger, yet she could do nothing but smile back at him.

'Hardly pursuing. But I can't find him.'

'No?' his mouth quirked. 'Give up on this fellow Lewis. I'd be happy to be pursued in his stead.'

Kate laughed. 'You? You're not the type.'

'What type am I?'

'I would have said that if there was any pursuing to be done, *you* would be doing it.'

'Beautiful *and* shrewd. I'm in the mood for a chase.'

He leaned back against the bench again, looking her over openly, appreciation in his grey eyes. Kate received the full impact of his appeal as if he had suddenly reached out and forced her to accept it. Physically he was compelling, with his broad shoulders and tapering body. Even in the immaculate blazer and slacks he looked athletic—a suntanned, outdoors man. He had straight, dark brows, a clean-sculpted nose and the perfect masculine mouth—wide with firmly moulded upper lip and full, squared off lower. There were lines around his eyes and a decisive firmness to his chin that put his age and experience at around thirty-five or even more, Kate thought. But whatever it was about him that held her there mesmerised, wasn't entirely physical. She didn't know how to describe the tension that twanged between them—didn't know how to account for the ridiculous thudding of her heartbeat because a stranger looked at her.

'What do you do here?' He looked at the clipboard of notes she hugged to her side, and she surfaced from her trance to realise that he thought she worked here.

'Nothing much,' she answered with perfect truth.

'I have to see someone, but I'll be free by two-thirty. Join me in the canteen for some of your excruciating coffee.'

It wasn't a question. Kate had the feeling that this man didn't often ask—didn't have to, perhaps. 'I'm in the mood for a chase,' he'd said. She told herself that she would refuse. She didn't make dates with strangers, however handsome and charismatic. She looked into his grey eyes. 'Yes,' she said, and had the incredible feeling that her answer might have been the same whatever his question.

His eyes let her go at last. 'Until two-thirty, then.'

She walked through the doorway, jostled by a woman who hurried past her into the mirrored room. In the corridor Kate paused to collect her senses. What was the matter with her? Her head whirled and she began to doubt that she had felt that incredible attraction to a complete stranger. She didn't even know his name—he didn't know hers. But the murmur of a deep voice inside the room reminded her that she had felt it. Her nerves fluttering with a different kind of anticipation now, she began to move away as the woman inside spoke.

'Have you been waiting long, Mr Beaumont?'

Kate kept walking down the long corridor and the name followed her, repeating mockingly in time to the clicking of her heels. Beaumont ... Beaumont ... she was suddenly, inexplicably bereft.

That was Robert Beaumont!

She had felt an instant bond with a man who had called her and Louise unethical and threatened them with legal action—with a man who was an arrogant snob. Kate stopped walking, found a door marked 'Ladies' and went in. With dismay she stared in the mirror at her hectically flushed cheeks, at the confusion in her green eyes, then glanced at her watch. She needed a few minutes to come to terms with this development in the faceless feud between herself and Robert Beaumont. Faceless—up until now.

Why couldn't he have been pasty-faced and paunchy? she cried inwardly, kicking herself for building up a false image of him. How could she have guessed that the annoying Mr Beaumont would not have the looks his acid tongue deserved? And how could she have let him suspend all independent thought? Had she considered it, she would have realised that a man waiting in the make-up room was likely to be making an appearance on television. She might possibly have made the next obvious assumption.

But she hadn't thought of it. Hadn't thought of anything at all but the embracing warmth in his eyes and the promise there.

She put up a hand to smooth the wisps of copper brown that clung to her neck. This wouldn't do. She had given the overbearing Beaumont an advantage, but she would have to pull herself together or he would make her look a prize fool. She had to put up some sort of a fight to show Beaumont that his status in the art world did not give him automatic rights to belittle

others less qualified. Some of the bemusement left
Kate's eyes. That was better. She would dwell on that
acid letter he had sent them and his lofty dismissal of
their venture as worthless.

Within months of moving into the cottage that they had
turned into 'Galerie Bowman' she had been heartily
sick of Robert Beaumont.

At the time they had wondered about the wisdom of
setting up their business only a mile from his prestigious
gallery. Not that the two establishments would be in
competition. Beaumonts had an established clientele, an
élite, monied clientele who could afford the exclusive
and very expensive art and sculpture that it offered.

'And we,' Kate had said, 'will be peasant by
comparison.' Their customers would find local paintings
and Louise's pottery at householder's prices. 'There's
no question of competition, Louise—we'll mind our
business and Mr Beaumont will mind his. He won't
even notice we're here.'

But he not only noticed but seemed inclined to take
exception after all. They had no sooner put up their
gallery sign than they received a concise letter from him
informing them that it was designed to mislead and, in
fact, duplicated his own. In the coldest terms he advised
them to remove it to avoid legal action. Kate saw red at
the tone of the letter, especially since they had never set
eyes on a sign of any sort outside Beaumont Galleries.
Ever since they had moved in their neighbour—though
abroad himself—had been throwing his money around
in re-landscaping and the sign had been removed for
alterations. But he was right.

When they went to look again at his elegant white
brick building with its immaculate gardens, the sign was
hanging in its proper place. It was amazingly like theirs.
Apart from a few flourishes it might have come from

the same hand. Even the names looked similar in the embellished script.

It had been demoralising. After two months of back-breaking work they had scarcely had time to celebrate the raising of their sign before they were taking it down. But it wasn't the disappointment of it that gnawed at Kate so much as the pompous attitude that Beaumont had taken. His swift assumption that their mistake was deliberate and his threats of legal action upset even Louise's mild nature but infuriated Kate.

And that wasn't the end of the man's negative interest in them. Kate looked again at her watch. It was time to go and find Mr Lewis. She looked in the mirror, nodded approvingly at the militant gleam in her eyes. The dreamy, eager look had gone completely, and she squirmed to think that Robert Beaumont had ever put it there. But he would find her very resistant to his lazy magnetism when next they met.

When she emerged into the shiny-floored corridor, a man overtook her, heading for the studio.

'Looking for someone?' he broke stride long enough to admit that he was Steve Lewis and gave her instructions. Kate couldn't help thinking how ironic it was. So elusive before, the man simply turned up now that she had made such a fool of herself in search of him.

Her heart was knocking at her ribs when she entered Studio One with a bunch of women who were part of the live audience. The backchat show was a popular afternoon programme that owed its success largely to the personality-plus host, Dave Scott.

With her hands tightly gripping her bag and notes, Kate hovered near one of the huge, unmanned cameras. When all the ladies had seated themselves she saw Robert Beaumont and the compère standing under the monitors with the floor manager, who was wearing earphones now and looking about for her. When he saw her he came over followed by the others, Robert Beaumont bringing up the rear, and Kate had the satisfaction of seeing him stop short as he saw her.

She levelled a cool gaze at him across the compère's shoulder as the introductions were made and her green eyes flashed a challenge. His brows drew together in a frown, his grey eyes unreadable.

'Well, well—I'm not sure that you're quite what I expected, Miss Bowman—Kate.' Dave Scott flashed his well-known smile. 'Have you met each other?' His glasses glinted as he looked from Beaumont to Kate.

'Just in passing,' she said, and her cool look at the tall, dark figure next to Dave was spoiled by the rush of colour to her cheeks.

Scott watched them curiously. 'You'll have a wait of maybe fifteen minutes before you're on. Relax in the soundproof lounge there and Steve will give you the nod during the commercial break.' He gave a chuckle as Kate turned to go. 'Try not to break the place up, hey?'

The noise of the studio was banished as Kate closed the door of the glassed-in room and sank into one of the plush visitors' chairs. Looking out at the untidy studio was like watching a silent movie, she thought, her eyes going to the men still standing outside. Robert Beaumont said something and Scott laughed, clapping him on the shoulder.

Old pals, by the look of it. Kate stoked the fires of resentment to quell the last-minute nerves that fluttered in her stomach. Robert Beaumont was the type who had influence everywhere apparently, even here. It was difficult to match his attractive face with the damning words he had written to the press. That was what had started this whole thing, of course. She wouldn't be here now, quaking at the idea of appearing on camera, if it hadn't been for Robert Beaumont's letter to the editor.

'. . . the public are being ripped off by the owners of many so-called galleries,' he had written. 'I know personally of at least one gallery'—and Kate had known he meant *them*—'recently set up by owners who have little or no knowledge of art.' He had gone on to accuse the unnamed culprits of charging exorbitantly for work completely lacking in artistic merit and finished by saying, '. . . Those dealers prepared to accept second and third rate pictures should have the grace to style themselves other than a "gallery". A suitable title might be "art-mart", which suggests the instant, stereotyped wall decorations they handle and would attract to them the customers they deserve, instead of wasting the time of those seeking genuine art.'

'*Genuine* art!' Kate had fumed. 'Who does he think he is? That pompous, smug . . .! How dare he say that we know nothing about art?'

'Calm down,' Louise advised. 'It's just possible that he doesn't mean us at all.'

'He means us, Louise. After that business with the sign, he must. The thing is, what are we going to do about it?'

'Nothing.' Her aunt was adamant. 'Just ignore it.'

And maybe, Kate thought, she would have done just that if she had known her reply would bring this in its wake. For reply she did, to the same newspaper, and as a result was here to give her views on camera. And that gave Mr Beaumont a considerable advantage. She was well aware that as a businessman and art critic of some standing, he would be used to interviews, and she was not. Deep down she quailed at the task she had set herself. The odds were heavily against Robert Beaumont retracting one word of his criticism.

But although their gallery had not yet proved itself, she had brought away with her one small private encouragement. A faint smile touched her mouth as the man on her mind came towards the glassed-in room. If he could see the painting that had been sold yesterday while she was out, his handsome mouth would drop open.

Both she and Louise had been amazed to find a buyer for the worst painting on their walls. For if Mr Barrett's ghastly gums sold, then everything else hanging in Galerie Bowman might eventually. She'd only agreed to hang it because the old man who painted it was too nice and too sick to refuse ... because she was soft-hearted, she admitted. Something that would never interfere with Robert Beaumont's judgment.

A burst of applause flowered and died at Robert Beaumont's entry. Pointedly she ignored him when he sat down beside her, giving her fullest attention to the studio outside while her mind seethed with fragments of his written insults. And to add to her confusion she kept remembering the sound of his voice ... 'I'm in the mood for a chase'.

'You haven't a hope, you know.' The deep voice was infuriatingly calm, even amused next to her, and Kate turned her head unwillingly towards him.

'You know the saying "fools rush in". You're a fool to take me on, Miss Bowman. And I can make you look exactly that.'

Kate felt a rush of temper and swallowed hard to crush it. She must not let this man trap her into being emotional. If she did that, he *would* make a fool of her—and Louise. She counted to ten before answering.

'Testing the opposition, Mr Beaumont? Were you hoping for an undisciplined temper to immobilise me?' Her green eyes were sparkling with contempt and her first taste of battle. She hoped he had no idea just how finely balanced her temper was.

'With that colour hair,' he ran an experienced eye

over her upswept copper hair and curling wisps at the base of her neck, 'it was worth a try.'

Kate began counting again. At this rate, she thought, it would be a triumph merely to appear on the show without losing her cool.

'It's always important with a woman to know how far she will go,' he went on, 'and how fast.'

His profile was turned to her, hiding his expression, but she knew he was slyly reminding her of her instant attraction to him in the mirrored room.

'Yes, I agree. It's so important to find one's rival's weakness.' She paused, added sweetly, 'But I did my reconnaissance a little earlier, didn't I?'

'Are you saying that you knew who I was when you walked into that make-up room?'

She shrugged. 'You are rather well known. You would hardly expect someone in the art world not to know you, surely?' If only she *had* known he was not the over-indulged figure she had conjured up!

'No,' he murmured, 'not someone in the *art* world.' He used her own emphasis and turned it into an insult.

Cool—keep cool, Kate warned herself, and her palm itched to make contact with his assured face. She had a sudden vision of herself on camera, reaching across Dave Scott to slap her rival, and gave a little cough of laughter at the imaginary scene.

'Something amusing?' Robert Beaumont's mellow voice said next to her.

As they rose in response to the floor manager's beckoning she smiled and said softly, 'I was just hoping I wouldn't have to hit you during the show, Mr Beaumont,' and was gratified to see him blink, his composure just ever so slightly threatened.

They went before the cameras and sat one on each side of a beaming Dave Scott as the audience obediently clapped. The chairs were grouped under a barrage of

lights and a boom microphone. The bulk of the cameras
closed in and Kate's stomach turned over at the
pressing paraphernalia of technology.

'Well, well,' Dave Scott burbled. His 'well, wells'
were part of his style. 'We've got quite a little war being
waged here!'

He read out one or two of Beaumont's comments
contained in his letter to the newspaper.

'That's how Robert Beaumont, art dealer, writer and
critic, sees it. And Miss Kate Bowman, part owner of—
ah——' he shuffled his papers, 'Galerie Bowman, said
this in reply——'

Kate listened, remembering how aggressive the words
had looked in newsprint. Deliberately she had copied
Beaumont's style and laced it with sarcasm . . . 'Even
without an awesome knowledge of spatial concepts,' she
had written, 'I and others like me can decide whether or
not a painting works. Though labouring under a dearth
of information on the subtleties of composition, tone
and harmony, we are able to tell almost at once if the
picture . . .' Louise had been shocked at her pointed
attack on Robert Beaumont. While he had made only
hinted reference to them, she had used his name boldly.
'I suggest that Mr Beaumont sticks to his élite market
of monied people who more often buy for tax purposes,
for status or for an investment.' Of course that wasn't
entirely true, but she'd been so mad at the time that
she'd made a black and white case of it. 'He is
supremely equipped to advise and supply people in this
privileged bracket. For the rest of us the question of
whether we like a picture will remain the top priority
when buying art. And who is to say if an amateur work
fulfils the criterion that it is not art?' She had added a
great deal more about arbitrary judgments and superior
attitudes and finished with a satisfying thrust . . . 'There
will always be art-mart galleries, as you term them, Mr

Beaumont, because there will always be people—
ordinary people—who do not understand, nor wish to,
the élitist snobbery of what you call genuine art!'

Kate's mouth was dry as one camera moved closer,
its light a mocking red eye. She held on to her courage
by looking across at Robert Beaumont who was leaning
back, at ease in his swivel chair. 'Anything you can do,'
she said to herself, and did likewise, forcing her
trembling hands into stillness on her notes and smiling
at Dave Scott.

'You two have really started something! The
newspaper has had dozens of letters supporting each of
you. When did you actually meet?' He directed the
question to Beaumont and his brows shot up at the
answer. 'Half an hour ago? Were you surprised to find
that the woman who termed you,' he referred to his
notes, '"an élitist snob" was a gorgeous girl?'

What sort of a question was that? Kate thought in
disgust. She should have realised that this kind of show
was inclined to be chattily entertaining rather than
informative. If she didn't take full advantage of her
opportunities to put her case, it could well disintegrate
into inanities. Though right now she wasn't sure that
she would be able to speak if she had the chance. Her
face was all but paralysed into a half smile for the
cameras.

Robert Beaumont answered in his deep, authoritative
voice.

'Women rarely surprise me. Many—gorgeous and
otherwise—have called me names, but I don't let it
bother me.' He leaned forward, looked across and his
eyes slid over Kate's face and down to her shapely legs
which were folded demurely to one side. 'But you're
right—she *is* gorgeous.'

The audience tittered and Kate's smile slipped. With
that look Beaumont had reduced her status to an

attractive female package just made to please the eyes of men. She gritted her teeth and anger gave her back her voice when Dave Scott turned to her.

'And what do you think, Kate, now that you've actually met the man? Is he what you expected?'

'No, not all. Up until recently,' she lied to cover that galling moment when she'd fallen under the spell of a man whose name she hadn't known. 'I was quite certain that Robert Beaumont was paunchy, balding and had a pasty face.'

'Pasty face?' queried Beaumont with a faint smile.

'From all that indoor work,' she replied promptly, and the double-edged answer raised his brows.

There it was again. A current ran between them as if the compère wasn't there. Almost tangible, it sparked from one to the other. The audience's middle-aged women leaned forward.

Dave Scott gave them both a chance to state their case. Kate, recovered now from her nerves, defended the artists whom her rival condemned, aware that she was somehow giving the impression that she knew nothing about art. Beaumont's stance had pushed her into championing mediocrity, which wasn't what she believed in at all. While far from his exalted heights, Kate had the benefit of some years of training in both painting and appreciation. And a year's work as assistant in a small gallery had taught her good from bad. She laboured to defend her original views while indicating that they sprang from tolerance rather than ignorance. But as she fell silent she wasn't sure she had succeeded.

Robert Beaumont was as articulate as she had feared and as arrogant as his letters—though not, she noticed, as pompous. He finished up, 'And though I wasn't aiming at Miss Bowman's place in particular, it certainly does represent the kind of establishment I dislike. It's not a gallery at all. It's a hobby shop.'

Dave Scott's head swung to her for her reply. She was counting again. 'Mr Beaumont seems hung up on semantics. Whether you call your place a gallery or a shop, Mr Beaumont, the fact remains that your clientele are more impressed by the signature on a painting and high, high prices. They will buy the most hideous nude scratched out in purple crayon provided it has a famous name to flaunt in their status game. Whether we call our place a gallery or a hobby shop, we display the work of budding artists because we know that there are plenty of people who want to buy pictures they like at a price they can afford and who are not concerned that what they buy is a masterpiece.'

'You're filling their homes with rubbish,' Robert Beaumont said flatly, but he was eyeing Kate's breathlessness with a certain amusement that sent her temper soaring.

'*They* don't think so . . .' she began heatedly, when Dave Scott intervened.

'Before we go any further, let's qualify just what is a "good" painting. I believe you've brought an example with you, Rob?'

Beaumont hesitated, looked at Kate. 'Yes, I have. But perhaps we haven't the time to discuss it. Miss Bowman might think I'm lecturing her on "genuine art", and I'd hate to bore a beautiful redhead.' He smiled almost teasingly at her. 'It would be such a waste!'

The audience laughed. Dave's eyes flickered from one to the other.

'You're wasting your expert charm on me, Mr Beaumont. If anything your lectures could only be less tedious.'

Kate heard the words rush from her mouth with astonishment. It was hardly surprising that Beaumont's smile was wiped away in an instant. She stuck her chin up a little higher. Good. She liked it a lot more when he stopped reminding her that he had held her in a helpless trance. There was nothing even remotely warm in his grey eyes as he indicated that he would after all deliver his 'lecture'.

'As Miss Bowman has so graciously invited me to continue,' he said smoothly as he was handed a wrapped picture, 'I've brought a sample of very poor work. The kind of painting that Miss Bowman hangs in her—ah—gallery. The kind with which she hoped, along with a very misleading sign, to lure clients. In fact,' he removed the paper and directed a hard look at Kate who had gasped at the picture, 'it *is* one of Miss Bowman's offerings, which I purchased at a ridiculously high price considering its intrinsic worth.'

It was the worst picture they'd had on their walls—the one that had so unexpectedly found a buyer only yesterday. Beaumont went on to clinically point out the faults in Philip Barrett's landscape. The beautifully shaped hands, tanned and capable, moved over the surface and his words tore it to shreds.

There was nothing Kate could do but watch and burn with humiliation and anger at what this would do to the old man who had painted it so enthusiastically. Not even the rankest amateur should have this public criticism thrust upon him. Beaumont seemed completely unmoved that it was the work of someone whose pride would be humbled by his condemnation.

She thought of Louise watching at home and felt a sudden desolation that she had brought this on her. It was all her own fault. Try as she would to stop them, tears prickled at her eyelids and glittered, dangerously near to falling. The alert cameraman zoomed in and she knew she had to see it through without falling apart. She looked down at her notes on the clipboard but knew that nothing she had written there was defence against this.

'It makes me wonder just how Miss Bowman can claim to know good from bad when she is prepared to hang something like this,' he concluded.

'I liked it,' she lied. 'That's why.'

He had her cornered by her desire to protect Mr Barrett. No one with a scrap of feeling would publicly declare that the picture had been accepted out of pity—especially after it had been so thoroughly condemned. And Kate could just imagine the double satisfaction that would afford Robert Beaumont—to expose her as a foolish, sentimental businesswoman as well as an art amateur.

'What is more, Mr Beaumont, I'm willing to bet that someone else will like it enough to buy it. We will refund your money for the picture and re-hang it. I'll bet it will be sold inside six weeks.'

Beaumont stared at the suspicious brightness of her eyes. 'And what will you bet me Miss Bowman?' he asked.

The studio audience stirred.

Kate's eyes shifted. 'I—er——' she hadn't expected him to take it literally, and the tone of his voice inexplicably quickened her pulse.

'If it isn't sold in that time, Miss Bowman, you can work for me at my place for a day and see how a real gallery is run.' He paused. 'And we'll compare notes over dinner.'

There was a gentle sigh from the onlookers.

'Well, well—that sounds fair enough to me.' Dave Scott rushed in to fill the small silence and somehow Kate found herself agreeing. 'Now, Kate,' the genial compere took her hand consolingly, 'don't worry too much about Rob's comments. I'm sure you'll be inundated with customers now that they've seen you.

Me for one. Ever been inundated by a compère, Kate?' he grinned, and his fans laughed, easing the atmosphere back to comedy. For everyone but Kate, that was. Her brain was reeling from the disastrous outcome of this appearance.

Dave Scott chatted on, the audience responded, and with a few seconds to spare Robert Beaumont leaned forward and said: 'You won't forget that you promised to have coffee with me, will you, Miss Bowman?'

'Eh-heh-heh—what's this? Did you?' cried Dave archly as he winked at the audience.

'Yes.' Kate was terse. 'But that was before I knew who he was.'

She bit her lip and glowered as she realised she had fallen into the trap. Robert Beaumont lounged back in his chair, a gleam of satisfaction in the grey eyes that watched her. Damn, damn, she cursed her quick tongue. Now he knew that that initial attraction had been genuine.

The segment wound up and Kate could hardly wait to leave. Outside the studio door Dave Scott said a hurried goodbye to them and Kate reached for her cheque book as he went inside.

'I'll take the picture back now, Mr Beaumont,' she clipped.

'By all means, Miss Bowman.' His voice held a smile that made her grit her teeth. She couldn't trust herself to look at him, but slapped the cheque into his hand and reached for the picture he was holding.

'Allow me to carry it for you,' he said, and began walking so that she had to follow. He didn't bother to look to see if she was with him. 'I'm heading home myself now—as my date for coffee has apparently been cancelled.'

Kate met his brief glance at her in stony silence and looked with loathing on the dark, waving hair and the broad shoulders. He strode at a fair pace and she had to lengthen her steps to keep up with him. Her eyes fixed on a spot just below his shoulder blades in the middle of his well-muscled back. She thought of Mr Barrett and wished she had a palette knife in her hand at this moment. It would be very therapeutic to lash out at Mr High and Mighty Beaumont. They reached the door and he turned around, looking down at her.

'You don't carry a knife with you, do you, Miss Bowman?'

Her eyes widened at this interception of her fancies. 'Unfortunately, no.'

'Must be my lucky day,' he murmured, and held the door open for her as she passed through, scrupulously avoiding the slightest contact with him.

Kate stared at another car while he put the picture in her van. Low-slung, sporty and white, she had seen it snarling up the road past their gallery. It had swept past the night she and Louise had been foolishly drinking a toast to their new sign—the sign that had come down only days later, prompted by Beaumont's righteous letter.

'Let's get one thing straight, Mr Beaumont. Louise and I did not copy your sign. It was pure coincidence that our lettering and name should look similar.'

'Obviously you didn't feel that would stand up in court or you wouldn't have removed it so fast after my letter.'

'But we'd never *seen* your sign! We'd driven past a few times, but . . .'

'Then you must have seen it and decided to make use of the name similarity. Beaumont—Bowman. Clients looking for Beaumont Galleries could easily think they'd been mistaken when they came first to Galerie Bowman—until they got inside, of course. But it was a clever move.' He paused. 'I suppose Bowman *is* your real name?'

Kate went white with anger. Almost she hit him, got as far as raising her hand but reached out instead and clenched her fingers around the edge of the open car door. His eyes followed her hand, saw the white knuckles and the tension in her wrist.

'Very wise,' he said softly. 'You must blame your own bad temper for your embarrassment in there, Miss Bowman. Hasn't anyone told you that conciliation is sometimes advisable instead of provocation?'

To her dismay, tears rushed to her eyes. She slid into the car seat and slammed the door on Robert Beaumont's arrested expression. As she drove away she looked in the mirror and saw him stride to his car. The views of Mount Coot-tha passed unseen and she was blind to the beauties of the Botanical Gardens that wrapped about the Planetarium at the foot of the mountain. It had been infinitely worse than she could have imagined. The earlier skirmishes on paper were mere pinpricks compared to today.

By the time she was halfway home, she was desolate. On a quiet stretch of road she pulled over and reached for her handkerchief and let her anger spill in a torrent of tears.

Between sniffs she said vengeful things about the cold, hard man who was their neighbour, using all the words that Louise hated to get them out of her system. With her head resting on the steering wheel she sat until the beep of a horn brought her chin up.

A white sports car slowed long enough for the driver to see her sit up, then sped around the bend and out of sight. Maybe he thought she had collapsed from the sheer strain of defying him, Kate thought.

A momentary recollection came to her of warm, smiling eyes and a voice as sensuous as a caress. Kate banished it, overlaid the astonishing clarity of the moment with Beaumont's disastrously simple humiliation of her. Colour flared in Kate's cheeks to rival the vibrancy of her hair. She started the car.

'I hate you, Robert Beaumont,' she said aloud.

CHAPTER TWO

THE drive back, along the dappled rising road, through patches of thick, palm-speared forests and open plateau farmland, would normally have soothed Kate. Today, the green and lovely lower reaches of the McPherson range failed to work their magic. Today her eyes stayed on the road and she blinked a little as she sped through patches of green shade to emerge into the glitter of sunlight.

When the forests ended, the open wooded land began, dipping and flattening into another plateau before the engine note of the little van changed, labouring into a new ascent. Tall hedgerows of wild tobacco and the nuisance lantana fringed incredible, wild views of plunging mountainsides and peak woolly with foliage and scarred with great faces of rock that would run with falls in the wet season.

The area was dotted with farms and hidden away behind the tall mountain timber were chalets and log cabins and A-frame houses. The mountains were a haven for artists and craftsmen and for the tourists who bought their wares as they passed through to the waterfalls and the ancient rainforests that rang with the calls of whip birds and pittas, and parrots. There was a magic about the mountains, and Kate and Louise had not been proof against it.

The empty cottage on its overgrown acre just five minutes from the village of Lindale had attracted them immediately. It sat—or, as Kate put it that first day, 'crouched' in the long grass and overgrown gardens, pressed in by untrimmed domestic shrubs and encroaching bushland.

'Louise,' Kate had said in dismay, 'stop me from instant sentimentality! I've got the awful feeling that we have to rescue it before it goes under.'

'You're asking the wrong person. I feel the same way,' calm, sensible Louise had replied.

The forlorn house claimed them both, and though on first sight it seemed a picturesque derelict, its timber was sound and the roof was intact. Only the neglected garden made it so down at heel.

'And that,' Kate declared in her ignorance, 'will be easy to fix.'

Nothing, it turned out, was easy to fix, but their back-breaking efforts on the cottage paid off. Emancipated from the press of growth around it, the house looked bigger, stronger.

'It's gaining confidence,' Kate announced after her first attack on the garden. With the vegetation tamed again, at the front at any rate, the brown-stained house began to rediscover its personality. The wide, closed-in verandahs became the picture and pottery galleries and the small rooms behind, their home and Louise's studio.

Kate turned into the drive beside their new sign that announced 'Galerie Bowman' in lettering as unlike Beaumonts as they could find. She parked the van at the side of the house and went inside, carrying Philip Barrett's picture in her hand and mortification in her heart. The business was half hers, but it was half Louise's too, and she had let herself be provoked into this exposure today. As a result the gallery could well become a laughing stock.

She found Louise in the kitchen, pouring coffee.

'I imagine you could use one,' she said, eyeing Kate with sympathy and a certain resignation.

'Well, at least I didn't hit him,' said Kate with a philosophical shrug, 'But I came close.'

'Hmm—he was rather harsh. But you weren't exactly a mouse yourself. I had my fingers crossed that you wouldn't lose your temper.' She sighed. 'I don't know why I agreed to it. As soon as I saw his face I knew he was intending to use Philip's picture . . . a pity I didn't know who he was when he came in yesterday.'

Yes, Kate thought, remembering her earliest stupidity today—it was a great pity.

'But, Kate, he was having second thoughts, I swear, until you were so . . .' She stopped at the desolate look on Kate's face. 'Yes, I suppose you've realised that by now.'

They went through to the gallery and Kate re-hung the picture and took her coffee from Louise.

'You were a mite quixotic, weren't you? Betting to sell this in—what! Six weeks?'

'No one will remember that.' Kate straightened the painting. It had all been bravado on her part to offset the old man's humiliation. Of course if she'd held her tongue he might not have been humiliated at all. But stubbornly she maintained that Robert Beaumont had no right to come sneaking in here to buy it in the first place.

'I suppose there's no chance of Philip not finding out about the backchat show?' she murmured in forlorn hope. At least a second-hand account of it from someone else would be less painful than actually seeing it.

'No chance, I'm afraid,' Louise said dryly. 'Andrew rang before you got back. His father saw the show and phoned him at work. According to Andrew he was very upset.'

Kate grimaced. 'I'll ring him tomorrow when I'm clear-headed again . . . I'm sorry, Louise. If I hadn't been so stupidly sentimental I wouldn't have agreed to take Philip's painting.' She looked glumly at it. 'But honestly, how could I refuse him? He looked so frail and he was so darned enthusiastic.'

'And of course it had nothing to do with the fact that his son is charming and extraordinarily good-looking.'

Kate smiled weakly. 'I didn't do it to please Andrew, though I have to admit I find both the Barrett men very likeable.'

'Yes, they are. But at least Andrew can paint.' Louise went to look at his three watercolours that hung nearby.

Andrew Barrett had been their first local painter to offer his work to them, and Kate had had no reservations about it at all. Or about Andrew himself, if it came to that. He was twenty-four or five, a couple of years older than her, almost too good-looking to be true and genuinely nice. The trouble was, he had brought his father along later, and he was genuinely nice too—and look what had happened!

'Kate,' Louise implored, 'after this, please, *please* forget about Robert Beaumont, whatever he says. We just don't need any more publicity.'

And that, Kate thought as she followed her aunt to her studio, was the extent of Louise's rebuke over the whole business. There would be no more reproaches and 'I told you so's', which only made Kate feel worse. Others might have felt justified in raising the roof about her foolishness. Her own mother, Kate knew, would not have been so tolerant. But then Fiona Malvern wouldn't even be on her side. Robert Beaumont's superior snobbery would be much more to her mother's taste.

With affection Kate watched her aunt seat herself and take a small block of clay, pushing back her brown hair in the gesture that invariably left powdery fragments clinging to her brow. Louise had been more than an aunt to her. When her parents divorced and her mother remarried, leaving Kate with her father, Louise had seen her through her puzzling teen years. Then when her father, Louise's brother, had died it had seemed natural that they make their home together.

At forty Louise was attractive but reserved and shy socially. Kate could never understand how a gentle, sweet person like her had not married, and her only probings on the subject had met a politely shut door. Her aunt was content to devote herself to her craft.

'My kiln arrives this week,' she said prosaically. 'I'll be firing my first batch in it at the weekend.' A pause. 'Max is coming up to help install it for me.'

'Is he now?' Kate grinned, drawn from her brooding. Max Winter ran the local art and craft supplies shop in Lindale's leafy main street. He was also on the Creative Arts Group committee which counted painters, potters and sculptors among its members. Louise had been using the C.A.G.'s kiln to fire her pottery, and Max had been more than helpful.

He was a potter too and some of his work lined Galerie Bowman's walls, along with Louise's. Max called in frequently to deliver materials to Louise from the shop or to discuss the group's activities with her as she was now a member.

'Max is very friendly. Does he give all his customers such marvellous service?'

'Well—no, I mean—I don't ...' Louise saw the laughter in Kate's eyes and looked away smiling. A faint colour tinged her cheeks. 'Interesting,' thought Kate and, satisfied, left Louise to her slip and glazes and went away to contemplate her own folly.

Max made one of his calls the following day, greeting Kate with his slow smile. Tall and gaunt, with a full beard, he always reminded her of a sepia photograph of an Australian pioneer. He was a very brown man, his skin leathered by sun and wind, and his hair and beard grey-brown with his forty-six years. He was a widower, and his children were grown up and far away. He had opted out of city life to indulge himself with his pottery and run his shop.

'I've brought you a present, Kate.' Max was always bringing presents. His customers from farms and smallholdings brought him samples of their produce when they called at the shop for their paints or clay. Consequently Max frequently turned up with eggs, a pumpkin or a sack of stable manure. But this time he put his hand into his twitching pocket and brought out a bundle of fur. A tiny kitten crouched there on his palm, its eyes huge and timid.

'I found it wandering on the road miles from anywhere. Probably abandoned,' he told her.

The skinny creature mewed faintly. It was a pretty thing—a pale tawny colour with touches of tortoiseshell. Kate reached for it, her face soft with pity for the big-eyed ball of fur. 'Thanks, Max. You've found the poor little thing a home.'

She carried it off to the kitchen and arranged rugs in a box and warmed some milk. While the kitten lapped it from a saucer, she stroked its tiny head, and noticed that a part of one ear was missing. The pitiful little scrap had made a violent start in life. It went to sleep almost immediately, after having investigated and sniffed the rugs to its satisfaction.

In the studio adjoining the kitchen, Kate could hear Louise and Max talking about the Backchat show. She watched the kitten for a few moments as it lay curled in sleep, its downy fur rising and falling softly.

'... wouldn't have meant it personally. He comes down hard on mediocrity as a matter of principle. ...' Max was saying when Kate rose and went through to the gallery as she heard a car stop outside.

She casually straightened a piece of pottery and

turned with a warm smile ready for her prospective customer. But it was Robert Beaumont who entered, hands in his pockets and looking much as he'd done yesterday in the studio.

Kate's pulses leapt and she battled to conquer a sudden wish to start all over again. What would happen if she simply held out her hand to him and said, 'You must be Robert Beaumont'? Would he smile the way he'd done that first time with lazy warmth and promise? Just for a moment her eyes lit with pleasure at the thought, but in time she remembered that there was more, much more to the attractive man watching her. And, she told herself with excessive heat, she didn't like any of it.

'Good morning, Miss Bowman,' he said, and smiled—almost smiled, anyway.

'What are you doing here?' she blurted out, and although she had spoken in a low voice, the words echoed rudely over the timber floors.

'I——' he paused and Kate might almost have imagined him to be choosing his words with a certain lack of confidence. If he was anyone but Robert Beaumont.

'We seem to have made a bad start, Miss Bowman ...' Kate blinked. Surely he wasn't about to apologise? But he went on, his eyes suddenly warm, 'No, that's wrong. We made a very promising start, didn't we? It was only after we met that things started going wrong.'

He would have to bring that up. Kate felt herself reddening.

'No. It was all wrong long before we met, Mr Beaumont.'

Robert walked further inside and looked around, his gaze resting a moment on Philip Barrett's picture. Her hackles rose as she waited for him to comment, but he said nothing about it as he came and stood near her. Too near. Kate edged away, her defiance wavering with his closeness.

'If we put aside our—er—differences—you'd have to admit that our first impressions were favourable.' He smiled and moved a little closer and Kate's pulses clamoured so that she forgot to back away. 'I know mine were,' he said softly, 'and I think yours were too, if you're honest about it.'

Kate moved hastily. She'd been fool enough to fall for this easy charm before, but then she hadn't known what he was like.

'Yes, they were, Mr Beaumont,' she shook her head sorrowfully. 'But there, I'm so much younger than you, and bound to make stupid mistakes. I've discovered that you're not the kind of man I'd even care to have coffee with, let alone . . .' she stopped as she saw the dead end her tongue had led her into.

Robert's eyes narrowed on her, much of his good humour dissipating with her insulting tone. 'Yes—let alone . . .?' he prompted, then expelled an exasperated breath. 'Kate, I didn't come here to argue. I came to say that perhaps I was a little hasty when I——'

'Oh, I wouldn't accuse you of being hasty, Mr Beaumont. There's nothing rushed about your flat condemnations. You just think you're so darned right about everything that you don't consider anyone else's opinions.' Her eyes flashed at him. 'And I'm Miss Bowman to you. Only my friends call me Kate.'

His face tightened. 'If your temper is always so knife-edged I wonder that you have any.'

'Probably more than you, Mr Beaumont. I may not be perfect, but at least I'm not cold.'

'And I am? Don't judge too soon. As for you—no one would make that mistake about you.' He glanced at her coppery hair, twisted carelessly into a knot and wisping about her face. 'Rather you have an overflow of—passions.'

She flushed at his choice of word. 'Where you're concerned I've only an overflow of dislike, Mr Beaumont.'

For disconcerting moments he studied her.

'Your tongue will lead you into big trouble one day, Miss Bowman. If you don't learn to tame your temper, someone else will do it for you.'

'You, Mr Beaumont? Be careful. Fire isn't kind to ice.'

'Ice is water—and water extinguishes fire,' he said. 'That's elementary, my dear Miss Bowman.' His gaze was mocking, but she could see his anger simmering.

'Not *dry* ice—that just makes a lot of useless fog!'

He was furious, she could tell, and she was jubilant that she had managed to get under that cool skin of his. Kate discovered that her equilibrium was restored when he was ruffled. She felt somehow . . . safer.

'You ask for trouble. Didn't yesterday teach you anything?'

She burned with half a dozen sarcastic replies to that, but she had no chance to make one of them.

Max and Louise came in from the kitchen and there was a moment of silence while they recognised the visitor. Max, of course, knew Robert, who was patron of the C.A.G. When Kate had received the invitation to appear on television Max warned her about Robert Beaumont's uncompromising stance on standards. It was a pity his warnings hadn't been a bit more specific, she thought. If he'd told them that Robert Beaumont was young and darkly handsome and possessed the kind of sex appeal that should be labelled 'Danger'— that might have been useful.

The two men shook hands and Max introduced Louise, whose face was a little stiff.

'We've made a poor start,' Robert said again.

'Perhaps I should have called on my neighbours before this.'

'You did—the day before yesterday, Mr Beaumont,' Louise glanced at the Barrett picture, 'and didn't introduce yourself then. That wasn't very neighbourly.'

Robert smiled ruefully down at Louise and Kate could see her aunt softening under his charm. 'No. I'm sorry about that. Your niece has just been pointing out my shortcomings. In fact I believe she was just about to throw me out.'

Louise looked startled, but a glance at Kate gave her a fairly accurate picture of the situation.

'Well, if you've come with an olive branch, Mr Beaumont, I'll be happy to talk to you and clear up a few matters. Will you have some coffee?' She steadfastly ignored Kate fulminating by the door. In fact all three of them ignored her as they exchanged pleasantries about the mild winter and the C.A.G.'s coming art exhibition.

Max left, and Louise walked with Robert around the pottery gallery while he picked up an occasional item to inspect. He was exerting himself to be pleasant and Louise was relaxing her reserve at a breakneck speed.

'Join us for coffee, Kate?' Her aunt turned and made an imperceptible move of her head, urging her to join in the peace talks. It would be easy enough to do, Kate thought, suddenly depressed at the thought of continued friction with Robert. But behind Louise, he was looking at her with the suggestion of a smile about his well-shaped mouth, as if he knew that he had manoeuvred her into a corner. Her chin went up.

'No, thanks. I've got—other things to do.' She might as well have said 'better things', for that was how it sounded. But she didn't care, she told herself as she brushed through the curtained hallway to the bedroom she shared with Louise. Quickly she changed into her oldest working clothes and went out into the tangled scrub at the end of their garden to hack down the long grass. 'Damn him!' she muttered as she heard Louise's quiet laughter, and struck out at the tall growth until the sound of a powerful motor growled from their drive.

'Really, Kate,' Louise was almost sharp, 'you might have made some effort to patch things up! It can't have been easy for him to call in here. We don't have to agree with his opinions in order to be on speaking terms with him.'

'I don't like him,' Kate said mulishly.

'That's very plain. But it's time you controlled your feelings. We're in business now Kate and have to accept that people like Robert are potential allies. Anyway,' she added, 'I find him very pleasant in spite of his past comments about us.'

Kate was shocked. She couldn't remember Louise ever speaking to her quite like that. But half an hour with Robert Beaumont and here she was treating her like a spoiled child indulging in tantrums.

Louise sighed. 'I am playing the heavy aunt today, aren't I? Let's not fall out over a man, Katie—people might talk.'

Kate smiled at that, reassured by her childhood name and relieved that the touchy subject was shelved for the moment.

'By the way, have you decided on a name yet?' Louise knelt beside the box and looked in at the kitten, which was almost entirely obscured by the blanket. As she tweaked the rug, the tiny creature stirred and turned its head.

'I thought—Vincent,' Kate grinned.

'Vincent? A bit weighty for a cat, isn't it?'

'What else could you call an art gallery's resident one-eared cat *but* Vincent?'

Touching the ragged ear, Louise laughed softly. 'Well, of course!'

Kate watched her stroke Vincent and felt a surge of affection for her. She owed Louise so much.

'Lou, I will try to be civil to Robert Beaumont if he calls again. But I can't promise to like him.'

Louise touched her arm briefly. ' "Civil" will be just fine, Kate.'

But civility was going to be a tremendous strain, Kate realised when she made her call to Philip Barrett at midday.

'Ah, Kate,' he said, 'I could have hurled myself off one of the lookouts when I saw my poor old effort on television. Lucky I can't get too far in my wheelchair, eh?'

'I'm sorry, Philip, we had no idea he would do that— and I'm afraid it's my fault that he . . .'

'Now, now, Kate, don't you feel responsible. I wanted to have something hanging in a gallery and— well, this is what's happened.'

'Anyway,' she said, cheerfully, wishing she could get her hands around Robert Beaumont's throat, 'it's hanging up again, and who knows, maybe this time we'll get a genuine buyer for it.'

The old man brightened at that. 'Thank you, Kate. Andrew's just come home for lunch and would like a word with you.'

She went through her apologies again with a subdued Andrew, but before he rang off he invited her to a party, and Kate's spirits rose. He obviously wasn't blaming her too much.

'On Saturday, at my boss's house,' Andrew told her, and she agreed readily. Andrew was always fun and she looked forward to Saturday night. But it wasn't Andrew who was in her mind but Robert Beaumont. Kate decided that if she was to be civil to the man, she should sort out her feelings about him once and for all.

But every time she tried confusion reigned, and she deferred the task.

It niggled at her through the next busy days. She went to see an artist who had contacted her about staging an exhibition of his work. Her trip down to the coast at Currumbin found a studio full of amazingly good oils.

Kate was enthusiastic though puzzled. 'Why us?' she asked. 'Why would you want to exhibit with us—our publicity hasn't exactly been positive of late.'

Evan Gale grinned. 'I'll be frank with you, Miss Bowman. I sell pretty well and get good reviews mostly—except from Robert Beaumont. I have nothing to lose by being associated with you and everything to gain. It's a good location for a show.'

Politely she pointed out that she had never heard of him or his work in the Brisbane galleries.

'I'm new here—just moved from Melbourne. Your neighbour is even better known down there.'

'Tell me,' Kate was curious, 'is he always so—so unbending?'

Evan Gale laughed. 'Sure. You aren't the only ones to have earned Rob's disdain.'

'Do you know him personally, then?'

'Yes. We get along just fine—as long as we don't talk about art.'

'You *like* him?'

'Don't confuse the artist with the man,' he told her. 'Rob's a friend. We just don't see eye to eye about my work. But I'll tell you this about him—he's scrupulously fair. He's even poured scorn on some of the big names who imagine they can get away with the occasional botched job because they've already made it. Some critics are sycophants—but not Rob.'

'You seem to be more than fair yourself, considering he's critical of your work,' Kate said dryly.

He grinned, waved a hand around the room, 'He's absolutely right about it, of course. He rubbishes it because he knows I can do better. But I got tired of living on prize money—so I decided to paint to sell. That's where we differ.'

'Yes, I see.' Kate pulled herself back to business and arranged for Evan to send her a catalogue of paintings in a month and offered a few tentative plans for her advertising and presentation.

'It's a pleasure to do business with you, Kate,' he said as she left, and Kate went away more confused than ever about Robert Beaumont, who seemed to find acceptance even from his victims.

There was so much to be done that she compiled a list of jobs. But she threw it away.

'It's too depressing, Louise. There's enough on that scrap of paper to keep you and me in bondage until we're old and grey!' So Louise went on building up her stock of pottery and Kate worked to keep the old house from collapse and did her best to stem the creeping tide of jungle at their back door. Once she plunged into it to find Vincent, who had begun to grow cockily confident with the application of a few meals and some attention. She caught up with him as he skittered in circles near a hitherto undiscovered wire fence. Kate picked up the kitten and leaned over it to peer through the scrub. This, she knew, was Robert Beaumont's land. And according to Max, somewhere across to her left was the house that the great man himself occupied when he wasn't away on one of his jaunts.

For Robert Beaumont had no need to live frugally in the back rooms of his premises as she and Louise did. He had built a magnificent house up a winding drive and behind his tasteful gallery. But though she manoeuvred carefully through the prickly undergrowth,

Kate couldn't see it. She picked her way out carefully,
certain that the long grass hid whole families of snakes,
and found herself pondering on Robert Beaumont's life
style. What did he do when he wasn't busy putting
people down? she wondered. Did he live up there all
alone? She stomped back to the house, annoyed to find
him on her mind again. Who cared, she muttered, what
the man did!

But sometimes at night, when she lay with Vincent's
furry shape curved near her feet, she would remember
the magnetism of warm grey eyes in an attractive face—
and the smile that had held such promise ... oddly
disappointed, she would turn over, dismissing the
stranger from her mind.

'Ease up, Kate,' said Louise to her as she came in hot
and dusty from the garden on Friday. 'Why don't you
paint? And I don't mean window frames.'

She grinned. 'I just might do that.'

Her paintings were good and getting better. At art
school she had been one of the more successful students
until her ambition to start the gallery with Louise sent
her out to a series of jobs in search of the experience she
would need. She had been lucky to land a job for a year
with a small gallery in between her office jobs. But
painting remained a satisfying part of her life, whether
making coffee for old Mr Hartmann in his gallery or
typing pages of boring reports. In the past two years
she had picked up two commendations in small shows
and sold several pictures.

Portraiture was what she really loved. Later, when
she had more time, Kate intended to paint Max. That
lush beard and nut-brown skin would be a fascinating
project. As she worked on a painting begun six months
earlier, she planned in her mind the portrait of Max.
That strong nose and the gentle, caring eyes—it
wouldn't be easy to capture the exact expression in

those grey eyes. Kate exclaimed and took up a rag to wipe away the slip of her brush. What on earth was the matter with her? Max had blue eyes, not grey.

The urban landscape developed under her brush, but try as she might she was unable to bring Max's face into focus. Grey eyes, a sculptured, imperious nose and a strong mouth—they were the features that mockingly obscured any others. Even Andrew's startling good looks eluded her, as she tried to put Robert Beaumont from her mind.

'Brother!' She put down her brushes and stepped back to view her work with an irritated frown on her brown. Yes, it was developing nicely. Even Beaumont might approve of the balance, she thought, then snatched up her paints and bundled them away crossly. Even this he had managed to intrude upon. Painting used to be a pleasure—a relaxation, but like everything else lately it had been spoiled.

But when Louise enquired about her session, Kate smiled and pretended it had been every bit as therapeutic as it used to be.

CHAPTER THREE

'WILL you be all right here by yourself?' Kate asked Louise on Saturday night as she waited for Andrew to call.

The older woman pushed back her hair. Her cheeks were a little flushed when she answered in her calm way, 'I won't be alone. Max said he'd drop in later.'

He certainly was around a lot lately, Kate thought, and smiled at the touch of colour in Louise's face.

'Good,' she said, and added with mock practicality, 'You'll be able to give the kiln a good going over.'

Louise looked startled. 'We probably won't be working . . .' she began guiltily, then saw Kate's teasing smile.

Andrew arrived and they took stock of each other in startled surprise.

'I've only seen you in jeans!' they both exclaimed. Andrew's mouth remained slightly ajar as he admired Kate. Her dress echoed the colour of her hair which she wore waving back from her face to fall shining around her shoulders. An austere gold choker about her neck gave an Eastern cast to her green eyes and moulded cheekbones. Her full, richly curved mouth added the warmth of coral to her exotic colouring and heightened the pale honey tan that lingered from the summer. The fabric of her dress clung to the curves of her breasts, sweeping in to the slim waist and tenderly out again over her hips. 'Kate, you look terrific!'

'You're rather presentable yourself,' said Kate, thinking it quite an understatement. Every time she saw

Andrew, she was surprised all over again. His blue-eyed, fair good looks were almost too perfect for this century. His face belonged on a Greek statue of a beautiful young athlete.

Andrew's boss, Clarry Henderson, was a bluff, overweight man of good humour and unpretentious manner, and his wife was pleasant, if a little stiff.

'Delighted to meet you my dear,' Clarry said, clasping Kate's hand in his beefy left and drawing her inside. 'Glad to meet someone who can give old Rob a run for his money!'

She was nonplussed until she realised he meant Robert Beaumont. Her heart skipped a beat and her senses sharpened. Quickly she scanned the grouped faces behind her host and hostess. If Clarry called him Rob he must know him well, she thought, and hoped that the night would not be spoiled by the critic's presence.

But he was not there.

The Hendersons' house was a breathtaking blend of ultra-new and cherished old. Chandeliers and a deep-piled carpet, velvet cushions strewn in a conversation pit, brocaded settees and sinuously modern chairs lived in harmony. Paintings and sculptures revealed the Hendersons as collectors. A big curved bar occupied a corner against a glass wall that viewed a rioting garden in the courtyard outside. A series of arches framed the motion of dancers in an adjoining room. Music rose above the voices.

'Am I imagining it, or do they look at me a bit strangely?' Kate asked Andrew after they had circulated and gone to sit on the bar stools.

'They've probably seen you on television, or heard about it,' Andrew reminded her, and she flushed.

She had forgotten about that. But so far no one seemed to resent her references about élite snobbery, or her determined attack on Robert Beaumont's opinions.

Clarry came and carried her off to 'have a look' at his latest acquisition. 'You don't mind, do you, Andrew my boy?' he beamed, and Andrew drifted towards the music and dancing as Clarry steered her to a painting.

'What do you think of this, Kate?' He fixed her with shrewd eyes. Clarry wanted to see for himself if she was as uninformed as his friend Rob made out. She thanked heaven for her years at Mr Hartmann's gallery.

'Raf Zador——' Kate studied the large abstract, 'he's well known for his ...' she began to say, when an unmistakable voice interrupted from behind.

'Getting some advice on your investments, Clarry?' Robert Beaumont enquired.

Kate turned to face him with all the caution of a wrestler facing an opponent. As her green eyes met his she felt a shock of awareness similar to the one she had experienced at their first meeting. His gaze faltered momentarily as it rested on the magnificent colouring of her face framed by the luxuriant, fiery hair, but he recovered and ran his eyes quickly down her body and back again in assessment, bringing a flush to her cheeks.

'We *know* you two have met.' She heard Clarry's voice edged with laughter and curiosity, but it was almost as if she was alone with Robert Beaumont. Gradually she became aware that they were the focus for many interested eyes and that clinging possessively to his arm was a blonde woman of voluptuous build and striking face. She was about twenty-eight or nine and seemed amused at Kate's continued silence.

Clarry introduced her as Sonia Marsden and the girl smiled languidly at Kate. 'I'm all ears, Kate,' she said with a spite-edged smile, and indicated the painting with one hand, inviting her to go on with her comments on this 'genuine art' and make an ever bigger fool of herself than she'd done already.

Kate's temper flared. 'Are you, Miss Marsden? Well, we all have our own little problems, don't we?' She looked with sympathy at the girl's quite average ear lobes exposed by the sleek hairdo, then moved her gaze from the startled Sonia to the man at her side. Robert Beaumont's mouth twitched.

'Don't let my presence stop you, Miss Bowman. Go ahead and give your impressions. I'm sure Clarry will be interested to have a second opinion.'

He was needling her, making it clear that he didn't take her opinions seriously.

'I believe I'll come back to this one. I haven't seen it before, and first impressions can be so awfully misleading,' she said with a defiant tilt of her chin at Robert Beaumont.

His eyes lingered on her hair a moment. 'They certainly can,' he agreed dryly.

Clarry walked off with her to view another of his acquisitions, and it was half an hour before Andrew came looking for her. Kate nearly embraced him in her eagerness to put space between herself and Robert Beaumont in a room suddenly smaller with his presence.

'Dance?' asked Andrew, and was gratified at her enthusiasm. As they crossed to the adjoining room, heads turned to watch them.

'Robert Beaumont is here,' Kate told him. 'I think everyone is waiting to see if this time I lose my temper and slap him.' Her palm itched.

'Then we'd better both keep out of his way,' said Andrew. 'I'm not sure that I like his style either!'

They danced disco-fashion for a while, then closer as the music changed tempo. Kate relaxed in Andrew's arms and felt her heartbeat return to normal.

'I've been looking forward to holding you like this, Kate,' he murmured in her ear, and Kate experienced a pang of conscience. She drew back, hoping that in her anxiety to escape seeing Robert Beaumont she hadn't given Andrew the wrong idea. The lighthearted relationship they enjoyed was one she valued.

'I wouldn't mind a drink,' she said, and Andrew left her sitting on a divan while he went to fetch one. She got up and wandered about, looking at a woven wall-hanging until a touch on her shoulder turned her, expecting to find Andrew with the drinks.

It was Robert Beaumont. He had his arm about her waist and her free hand clasped before she could recover and they mingled with the other couples dancing. Curious glances followed them and Kate's cheeks grew warm. She stayed stiff and silent, refusing to look at the dark face so close to hers. His arm was firm, yet he held her so that their bodies didn't touch. Even so she could feel her skin tingling as if they were pressed close.

'I like your hair that way,' he murmured after a while.

'Oh, I'm so glad,' she replied sarcastically, and felt his hold tighten fractionally as he looked down at her. Stonily she stared over his shoulder.

'It was meant as a genuine compliment, Miss Bowman.'

And why that should affect her so, Kate couldn't think.

'I don't want your compliments Mr Beaumont.' How rude she sounded, she thought. Words just seemed to rush involuntarily to her lips when he was around.

'Apparently not.' He paused and she forced herself to remember her resolution to be civil to him.

'Did you come with that beautiful young man?' he enquired, and any civil remark she might have made was ousted by anger at his vaguely insulting description of Andrew.

'Yes. He is good-looking, isn't he?' she retorted, looking up at last into his face. Her heart gave such a jolt that she rushed on into speech. 'And he's all man.'

'Ah, I see. A dancing partner—and a sleeping partner as well?'

Her already pink cheeks were fiery now. So that was how he interpreted her reaction to him that first time! He thought she was one of today's liberated girls. And so she was, but not in that sense.

'I haven't known Andrew that long,' she said hastily.

'Strange, Miss Bowman. I had the impression that you made up your mind very quickly.' His voice was low and resonant, drawing her eyes back to his so that she felt like a butterfly pinned to the wall. He wasn't going to let her forget her initial response to him.

'Sometimes,' her tongue ran on rebelliously, ignoring the curbs she tried to put on it. 'Andrew might be next, but at the moment I sleep with—Vincent.' It was true, the kitten slept on her bed every night. She fluttered her eyelids a little. 'You wouldn't have met Vincent. He's—well, you might say a vagrant really. Not the type you would meet. But we took him in and he lives with us. He's very young and very—grateful.'

She disgusted herself with the stupidity of her words, but she wanted to do or say something to stop the awful awareness of him that wove its spell around her. She didn't care what he thought. Let him think she wasn't choosy, then he would have no reason to believe that her first reaction to him was anything special.

His expression was odd and Kate couldn't have said what he was thinking. For a few moments he pulled her close so that she was crushed against him. 'You're making a mistake to pick on anyone too young. You'll walk all over an inexperienced man and you won't get any satisfaction from that. Your intuition was in better working order that day at the studio.'

Heart pounding, Kate tried to pull away from him. He held her easily and murmured, 'Just say the word.'

'There's nothing I have to say to you, Mr Beaumont, that could be said in one word.'

'Liar. You made the perfect one-word answer to me the first time we set eyes on each other.' He moved his head back a fraction and Kate stared into his eyes. 'You said "yes".'

Later, much later as she lay in her bed, Kate wished she had hit him then. He had known it too and had held her even tighter for a moment. 'Don't try it,' he warned her, his face relaxed and faintly smiling as if he was merely discussing the music or the extravagant food provided by the Hendersons.

She had wanted to leave when the music stopped, but stubbornly feigned enjoyment and danced with Andrew as if he was the only man in the world. It was hardly surprising that he had kissed her goodnight without his usual restraint. Kate turned over and hunched under the bedclothes. Her uncomplicated relationship with Andrew had moved into new territory, and all because of Robert Beaumont.

'Arrogant pig!' she muttered, and thwacked the pillow with her closed fist. The man had permeated almost every part of her life. Now she had even used Andrew to cover her confusion. The kitten moved at her feet and she screwed up her eyes in embarrassment. She had actually said all those stupid things about Vincent and let him think . . . damn! Pulling the pillow over her head, she tried to sleep. And some time near dawn, she did.

If Louise wondered what brought on the whirl of

activity that followed, she didn't say so. But Kate cleaned, repaired and gardened with such urgency that her aunt finally ordered her to take a break.

'Take a day off—finish your painting and put it in the C.A.G. Show.' She regarded Kate thoughtfully. 'And that's an order.'

'Aye, aye, sir,' Kate giggled.

'And Kate—about the competition. Robert will be judging it.'

'Oh.' Kate's face closed. 'In that case . . .'

'For heaven's sake don't let that stop you entering!' Louise put her hands on her hips in exasperation.

'There's no way I want him casting those critical eyes over my work. Besides, he's only human—I think—and he couldn't possibly view something by Kate Bowman without prejudice after all that's happened. Not that I imagine I'd be among the prizewinners, but I would like to be judged impartially.'

Her aunt shook her head. 'You're underestimating his objectivity, I think, but never mind. Sign another name—it's that simple.'

Kate liked the idea. She finished the painting and hunted about for a name, eventually signing it B. Ransome.

'What does the "B" stand for?' asked Louise.

Kate shrugged and laughed. 'I've no idea. Beryl? Brian? I'm remaining anonymous *and* sexless. And Louise, I'd rather you didn't tell anyone that this is mine, not even Max.'

'If that's the way you want it, I won't breathe a word about my niece, B. Ransome.'

Kate left the painting in Max's shop with an entry form signed 'Ransome' and an address, equally anonymous, care of the Post Office.

And a week later she was critically surveying it along

with all the other entries at the C.A.G.'s show opening.
The auditorium, hired for the exhibition from the
school, was crowded, noisy with greetings and laughter
as the guests drank the free champagne. Louise had
gone off in search of Max and reappeared with a tray of
glasses.

'I've been drafted as a waitress,' she said cheerfully,
and paused long enough to point out Robert
Beaumont's gallery manager. 'Over there—Ben
Strickland.'

Kate looked at the pudgy man who lifted a pale hand
to smooth back his thinning hair. He was vaguely
familiar, but she knew she couldn't have seen him
before. He turned his head and caught their eye, then
looked quickly away, his forehead pleated into
permanent anxiety.

'Yes, he looks as if he works for Robert Beaumont,'
Kate said dryly.

'Remember, Kate, if you see Robert tonight—
civility!'

Louise went off again, leaving Kate to eavesdrop on
a couple who were discussing her picture and then to
reflect that it was true that listeners never hear good of
themselves.

Andrew was here tonight, on duty. He was stationed
at the door with a pretty brunette who laughed at every
other word he uttered, and Kate was glad to be able to
wander about alone.

The winning pictures were as yet unlabelled, so she
took a small notebook from her shoulder bag and
jotted down her choices for the winners' placings. It was
something she often did—a kind of game to see if she
had understood all those classes in theory and
appreciation. This time she was consciously trying to
see them through Robert Beaumont's eyes.

'Made your choice, Miss Bowman?'

Robert had come up soundlessly, yet Kate wasn't entirely surprised to find him beside her. It had been inevitable—another meeting with him. She turned her head and looked at him. His dark hair was brushed back and crisply waving, a hint of grey in the groomed sideburns. She hadn't noticed that before. He was wearing dark slacks and a tailored cord jacket. A cream polo-necked sweater in a fine, silky knit hugged his broad chest and emphasised the strong cast of his face. Her image of a pasty, overfed man couldn't have been further from reality. He was extraordinarily attractive as he stood there silently running his eyes over her figure in the snug velvet jeans and clinging sweater.

'Yes, I have,' she said, and tilted her chin in defiance. Although she wore very high heels he still had an advantage in height.

'I'm sure all the homespun artists wish you were the judge and not me,' he remarked. 'Your choices I'm sure would delight them.'

'I know the difference between good and bad, Mr Beaumont. And I could make a fair guess at *your* choices.'

'And how could you possibly do that? Woman's intuition? Or maybe you have a crystal ball?' His mouth curled in sardonic amusement.

'If I had a crystal ball, I would have stayed away from *your* part of the country!' she flung back, and reached out for a glass of champagne from a passing tray.

He did the same and raised his glass to her. 'That would be a pity. You're a very enlivening influence—if a rather uninformed one.'

The champagne tipped dangerously in Kate's glass. 'The trouble with you is you're too damned complacent! I'll bet I can pick at least one of your winners, Mr Beaumont.'

One dark, straight eyebrow rose. 'Another bet, Miss Bowman—rather rash, isn't it? You haven't won the last one yet. Or have you managed to unload that—er—unusual painting yet?'

'Not yet.'

'And what,' his eyes wandered over her copper hair, highlighted by the overhead lamp, 'are you risking losing this time? Make it worthwhile, because I'll certainly win this one.' He paused. 'A kiss, perhaps? That wouldn't be too much to lose for a girl who takes in grateful vagrants.'

She was angrily silent, about to say something but conscious of a group of people passing close by. The grey eyes lingered on her parted lips, still glistening with champagne.

His voice was low and confident. 'Yes, I think a kiss.'

Kate reached into her bag, nearly overbalancing her drink in the process, and took out her notebook. She tore off the sheet on which she had jotted her choices for First, Second and Third, and folded it twice. Then she tucked it into his jacket pocket, snatching her hand back from the warmth of him.

'You're on, Mr Beaumont. But what I want to know is, what do *I* get when I win?'

He looked at her insolently, murmured, 'What would you like? I'm yours to command.'

She raised her glass. 'That'll do,' she said flippantly. 'Mine to command.'

He moved away with a mocking incline of his head and Kate regretted the silly words. They sounded almost intimate, and judging by the warm assurance in Robert Beaumont's eyes, he thought so too.

Kate listened for the prizewinners' names with avid interest. Robert himself was making the announcements and his eyes met hers briefly from the dais. She was so tense with the wish to hear her own choices among the winners that she failed at first to register another even more important.

'B. Ransome—Highly Commended,' the deep voice said, and Kate blinked. With difficulty she kept her face quite calm, not looking at Louise across the crowd, but a slow warmth built in her with the full realisation of the distinction. The superior Mr Beaumont had commended her work. Hers! The uninformed woman who couldn't tell good from bad.

She raised her champagne to her lips to hide her jubilation as Robert Beaumont suavely finished his announcements, including two of the names on her list. This was quite a night, Kate thought, and watched closely as he handed the microphone to someone else and stepped aside to take a tiny piece of paper from his pocket. How very satisfying to have topped him, twice! One he didn't even know about yet—but he would, one day. His quick frown and search for her completed Kate's elation. She met his eyes above the crowd and thrust her chin in the air, then turned away with a light, 'I told you so' step.

But minutes later Robert found her and steered her into a quiet corner with a steely hand she couldn't shake off.

'How does it feel to be on the losing side for a change Mr Beaumont?' she enquired.

'Come on—admit you got the names from Max.'

'What?' She stared at him.

'I judged the competition yesterday and Max had the winners' names to make out the cheques. Confess—you already knew my decisions.' He was smiling as if he'd found her out in a practical joke. 'Clever of you not to put them all down correctly.'

'I swear, Mr Beaumont,' she gritted through a clenched jaw, 'if you say another word I'll toss this champagne in your face! My choices were just that. You're a poor loser.'

She strode away, setting her glass down angrily on the first table she saw.

'I'd like to leave now, Louise,' she said when she found her aunt.

Louise's glance went quickly to where Robert stood talking to several guests, then back to Kate's ruffled face.

'So soon?' she replied mildly. 'Go if you want to, Kate. Max will drive me home when we've helped clear up. Oh, and,' she lowered her voice, 'congratulations, Beryl!'

The drive home cooled Kate's temper a little. Robert Beaumont might refuse to believe her judgment but there was no way he could deny her other success tonight. She was going to enjoy seeing his face when he knew that she was Ransome. As she turned into the driveway, Kate gave a little laugh of pure excitement. But she admitted to herself, moments later, that it wasn't just the idea of scoring off him that thrilled her. She was disgusted to find that she was pleased he had liked her work. Which rather made a mock of all her fine words about his arbitrary pronouncements on art.

It was still reasonably early—only ten o'clock—and Kate shed her jeans and sweater for a pair of lounging pyjamas. They were softly draped peach jersey, old but very comfortable. Barefooted, she padded to the kitchen to make coffee. While she drank it she lined up her paintings and looked critically at them, Vincent prowled into the room and sat looking unblinkingly at them with her.

'What do you think, Van Gogh?' she murmured to him. But he looked at her disdainfully and began to wash himself.

For half an hour she stayed there, wondering what Robert Beaumont would think of these paintings, then stacked them up and went to the kitchen, followed by Vincent, who dived off after some elusive prey.

A knock at the front door sent her to open it, thinking that Louise and Max had finished rather early after all. She unlatched the door and pulled it open to find Robert Beaumont standing there. On impulse she tried to shut it in his face, but he was too fast. He put out an arm and leaned his weight against the timber, until he stepped over the door ledge and inside.

'How dare you push your way in here at this time of night!' she spat at him. 'You may be able to throw your weight around up the road, but this is *my* home!'

He looked down at her and she was suddenly uncomfortable in the clinging silk jersey pyjamas and bare feet. A dull flush started in her cheeks. Kate was still holding the door open and now he reached out, inexorably using his strength to shut it.

His gaze swept over her, taking in the curves of her hips and breasts, lovingly moulded by the soft material of the pyjamas.

'Am I interrupting something?' he asked, and glanced behind her to the curtained hallway. 'Were you about to—entertain the young and grateful Vincent?'

CHAPTER FOUR

KATE exploded. Her hand lashed out and caught him across the cheek, forcing his head to turn. The sound of the slap echoed across the timber floors and she was breathing fast as his head swung slowly back. His eyes were flint and his mouth a thin line.

Through all their clashes, she had never seen Robert really angry. And she was daunted—her eyes widened as she began to back away from him. Relentlessly he came after her, with the red mark of her hand on his face. She had wanted to see it there—had dreamed of it—and now it looked somehow shocking. Her own violence alarmed her and the look on his face made her abruptly aware of her vulnerability.

'I warned you not to do that!' he ground out when she was forced to stop, her back against the wall. With hard hands he pulled her to him and she gasped at his roughness. He raised a hand and she quickly averted her face.

'Oh no,' he assured her, 'I won't hit you. But you might prefer it.'

His hand went to the back of her head as he spoke, gripping her hair to tilt her face to his. Just for a moment he glared at her, then lowered his head to kiss her. It was something outside Kate's experience. She had been kissed before—tentatively, passionately, inexpertly—but never like this. His mouth was hard and bruising and his arms tightened about her until tears of pain and rage ran down her face. She struggled and kicked, and only succeeded in hurting her unshod toes, and still he kissed her, only raising his

56

head when he felt the wetness of her tears touch his skin.

He studied her distressed face and abruptly let her go, his mouth curling.

'I'm as bad as you—letting my temper go like that.' Ruefully he put a hand to his face and turned away from her to walk back along the gallery. She did not move but watched him until he turned and said, his voice reverberating in the room, 'I apologise.'

Silence. Kate tried to get a grip on herself.

'I came to talk to you, not terrorise you. It *is* quite safe to come near me. Can we sit down somewhere for a few minutes?'

Kate was so astonished by this unexpected conciliation that she moved forward. But her bare feet slowed as she came closer to him.

'We can sit in the kitchen,' she said grudgingly, and led the way.

He followed her and sat down at the scrubbed wood table, looking around at the bright home-made curtains and polished wood floors.

The small room seemed to shrink further with him in it and Kate was conscious of a new wariness as he studied her seriously for a few still moments.

'You really did predict my first and second placings?'

'I said as much, didn't I?'

'Then you've been misleading me about your qualifications. You must have had some training.'

Kate recovered at last. 'Such ego, Mr Beaumont! I've agreed with you, therefore suddenly I must be qualified. Suddenly I must have had training! I've agreed with Robert Beaumont and am ignorant no more!'

His mouth tightened. 'What a nasty tongue you have, Miss Bowman. It's a good thing for your business that your aunt is nothing like you.'

With rising fury Kate demanded: 'And what are you insinuating now? That I'm an undesirable type to have around but my aunt brings some respectability to the firm? Who the hell do you think you are?'

He crossed his arms and watched her, his face relaxing strangely enough at her outburst.

'I'm sure you're going to tell me, Kate. But do you think you could do so over a cup of coffee?'

She stopped in her tracks at his use of her name. 'Don't say that,' she said flatly.

'What? Coffee? Oh—er—then what about tea? Or cocoa?'

She looked stupidly at him.

'A glass of water?' he said hopefully, and an unwilling laugh left her lips. But her thoughts were in turmoil as she went through the ordinary motions of making the coffee.

'There was another reason I had to see you tonight, Kate.' She felt that peculiar pang again when he said her name. 'I came either to pay up or to claim my winnings.' He waited for her to say something, but she just stared. 'It seems you've won—and I always pay my gambling debts promptly. The trouble is, you're going to have to tell me how to do it. I'm yours to command, if you remember.'

He was actually teasing her, amused at it all. Something told her that he had interpreted her flippant words in quite the wrong way. Kate was tempted to play along just a bit—but not with the end result that Mr Beaumont might imagine. He clearly anticipated enjoying the payment of this debt.

She raised guileless eyes to his face. "Mine to command." Did I say that?'

'You hadn't forgotten,' he said, smiling with such assurance that she longed to toss her coffee at him. It was as if he knew she would command him to do something very pleasing. She wondered what he would say if she commanded him to wash the kitchen floor.

From the increasing warmth in his eyes, Robert wasn't expecting anything like that. Kate hesitated. If she misjudged her timing she could end up in deep water. But the desire to wipe that confident smile from him was too strong. She would risk it.

'No,' she said softly, looking him straight in the eye, 'I hadn't forgotten—Robert.'

She almost laughed, at the little flare of triumph in his eyes. Yes, the arrogant man had assumed too much.

He reached out a hand and covered hers where it lay on the table. With deliberation he lifted it and traced the outline of her palm with his thumb. The tiny caress sent staggering vibrations through her and she thought in panic that she would have to finish it soon while she was able.

The kitten padded into the kitchen and miaowed for attention, rubbing itself against first Kate's, then Robert's legs. Still holding her hand, he looked down briefly, then, his attention caught, looked again.

'He has one ear,' he said, and fixed Kate with an intent look that turned to amusement. 'Could this be the young vagrant, Vincent?'

'You made me angry that night,' she said shyly, hating herself, 'and I twisted the truth a bit. But he does sleep on my bed.'

The grey of his eyes warmed up another tone and she wished she hadn't mentioned 'bed'.

'We're alone, then,' he murmured. Without haste he rose and came around the table to her. Now, Kate thought—now was the moment to disillusion him. He took her hands and pulled her to her feet. She would tell him to go in just a moment . . . her mouth opened to repulse him, but somehow she was in his arms, pliant and willing, and the only sound she uttered was a sigh. And after a moment she forgot anything at all but the silken, seducing feel of his hands on her through her clothes and the persuasive touch of his mouth on hers. The pressure of his lips changed, moving warmly one moment, barely touching the next, until her head spun in multi-coloured space. Gradually his coaxing became demand and he parted her lips to begin a new seduction.

Kate clung to his shoulders, reeling as she tried to hold some coherent thought. At last he stopped and she was able to remember why she had let this happen.

'Isn't this better than fighting?' he breathed into her ear, while his hands roamed possessively over her hips.

She had a sudden vision of those hands moving over the surface of Philip's picture while he verbally tore it apart. Tilting her head to look into his eyes, she put up a hand to his face as if unable to resist him. And it was almost true. Almost. Her fingers caressed the faint mark of her angry hand on his cheek.

'Shall I tell you what I'd like, Robert?' she said softly. 'You're mine to command, remember?'

His eyes were dark slate with desire, a faint colour stained his tanned face and the sensuous masculine mouth was curved in the smile of the obliging lover. Yes, he would do whatever she liked. Kate couldn't take her eyes from him. She had him just where she wanted him.

'Tell me, Kate,' he urged, and bent to nuzzle her ear.

'I want you,' she whispered, 'to take your arrogance,' her voice raised to normal speaking level, 'and get out.'

There was a shocked silence as if he couldn't believe the words she had said. It was a moment before his body stiffened and his caressing hands turned to steel around her arms to put her from him.

'I—see,' he said in a voice like gravel. 'Revenge is sweet, is it, Kate? But don't try to pretend you were acting—not all the time. With a little effort I could carry this to its natural conclusion, and you know it.'

Inside she was shaking, but she forced a retort. 'You disgust me! On the one hand you want to put me down because I dared disagree with you, and on the other you're quite hypocritical enough to want—to want to——'

'Not baulking at the truth, surely, fearless Kate? Sleep with you—that's what I wanted to do.' His words were harsh and deliberate. 'Like most women you're prone to confuse the issue. But we both know what we've been heading for since we set eyes on each other. Because you had some trivial reasons to dislike my dealings with you, you conveniently exaggerated them to camouflage that very earthy response you showed me the first time we met.' He stopped abruptly, flicked angry eyes over her and his tone was calculatingly insulting. 'I could have had you right there in that make-up room, with a little persuasion.'

She blanched. 'You're over-confident, Mr Beaumont. I wasn't that impressed. And don't imagine I enjoyed one moment of your varied performance tonight—I found your expert seduction just as loathesome as your uncouth attack on me earlier!'

'No. We both know that's not true, Kate.'

His temper showed signs of abating, and Kate found that less comforting than she would have thought.

'You'd better leave, Mr Beaumont.'

At the door he turned suddenly and walked along the gallery, looking at the paintings one by one. He stopped at last in front of Philip Barrett's picture and tipped his head towards her where she waited by the door. 'This is one bet you won't win.'

'Time will tell,' she said, and her heart pounded as he came back, footsteps echoing on the floor. The spotlights on the gallery walls created shafts of yellow light between the soft-edged shadows. Robert walked through them, his dark face alternately highlighted and thrown into moving shadow and he looked powerful, formidable. But there was no anger left on his face when he stopped beside her. Rather he looked as if he had come to some decision, and his regained assurance bothered her more than his fury.

'This is just a skirmish, Kate. I intend to win the battle.'

She flung the door open and the cool night air rushed in. Unable to trust herself to speak, she slammed it shut as soon as he passed through. Motionless, she stood listening to his car door open and shut, the powerful motor turn over and hum its way down the short drive and up the road. Almost she fancied she could hear the change in its tone when it turned into the driveway of Beaumont Galleries nearly a mile away, to sweep beyond to his house.

The timber cottage was disapprovingly quiet. It was almost as if its old frame had been shocked into silence from its groans and creakings, by the ugly scenes enacted within. Kate moved to the kitchen and cleared away the two coffee mugs. She ran water into the sink, laced it with detergent and washed the two items in four inches of foam. Vincent rubbed himself on her ankles and she put out some milk for him, murmuring absently to him as he lapped it.

She felt hollow. The encounter had shown her a side to herself that she had never seen, and she loathed it. Self-disgust settled in her stomach and she felt physically sick. The conflict that had built up from its small beginnings had finally erupted into battle.

Her mind had not changed. Robert Beaumont was all the things she had called him on every occasion, but Kate knew that she would have to go to him and apologise for her behaviour nevertheless. Nothing else would make her feel clean again. She went to bed and feigned sleep when Louise came in, until at last she dropped into welcome unconsciousness in the early hours of the morning.

The older woman was already up and in her studio before Kate emerged from the bedroom the next morning. Louise hummed as she worked and it was clear that for her at least, the previous evening had been successful. Her face was serenely contented as she left the wheel and cleaned up to eat her usual light breakfast, although she spared a rather considering look at Kate.

'Good morning, B. Ransome,' she said. 'You left too soon last night. Your painting was sold.'

'So soon?' Kate's mouth dropped open, 'I can't believe it!'

'The sold sign went on just after the Highly Commended. Are you pleased that Robert liked your picture?' Louise added with curiosity. No doubt Louise would expect her to be elated at the bestowal of his approval and the subsequent sale of the painting—and she was. But last night's scene rather took the edge off it all.

'Sure. It's great.' Kate forced a smile to her mouth. 'But I don't want him to know it's mine—not yet.'

'Kate ...' Louise's tone was one of warning. 'Now you're not going to do anything silly, are you?'

'Of course not. But you can't blame me for wanting to use this, can you—after all the rotten things he said about us, about *me*, on television?'

Louise viewed her over her coffee. 'You should spend more time painting, Kate, and less time fuming over Robert and what's past. I had a chat with him last night and we sorted out the business of the sign at last. He knows we couldn't have copied it now.'

But Kate had had a chat with him last night too, and far from clearing up misunderstandings had only found more reasons to dislike the man and he had ended up anything but friendly. This could be very awkward, she thought suddenly, with Louise warming to him and herself cooling all the time.

'You like him,' she said flatly.

'Yes, I'm afraid I do.' Louise sounded faintly amused. 'Sorry about that, Kate—there's no accounting for tastes.'

'It's not funny, Louise. He's been insulting to us in the past and I can't imagine why he's suddenly turning on the charm.' Kate crossly stirred her coffee.

'Can't you?' Her aunt reached for the marmalade.

'He certainly turned it on with a vengeance when he called—all that gentlemanly courtesy and that—that smile he puts in his eyes.' She'd seen it there for her, too that first time, and even last night he had smiled that mind-spinning smile for her in between his anger.

'It is rather attractive, isn't it? I didn't think you'd noticed.'

Kate looked sharply at her aunt, who met her eyes in bland innocence. She decided that Louise's mind was on other things—Max, for instance. That probably accounted for her odd expression. She couldn't possibly think that Robert—she and Robert—Kate gave a snort of annoyance and cleared away the breakfast things until Louise was left with a slice of toast and the local newspaper.

'He said he'd drop in to see us one day,' said Louise from behind the pages, and Kate slammed a cupboard door shut. But he'd said that earlier last night.

'He won't.' Kate sounded so certain that the older woman lowered the paper to study her.

'Why do you say that?'

'Oh——' she couldn't repeat that unpleasant scene from last night, not even to Louise, 'He knows *I* wouldn't welcome him here.' Even as she thought about it again she remembered uneasily his parting words—'I intend to win the battle.' In the bright light of day the words had a melodramatic ring to them—yet Robert Beaumont didn't seem the type to indulge in dramatic effects.

So what did he mean?

The question rose again a few days later when Louise told her that he had called.

'Robert dropped in while you were out.'

'And my stars predicted misfortune,' Kate answered in cheerful sarcasm. 'I knew I couldn't be unlucky *all* the time!'

'You provoke a great deal of your misfortune, Kate. If you bit your tongue now and then you could make a friend of Robert. *He's* trying.'

'Now there I agree with you, my dear aunt. He *is* trying—very trying!'

'What is it with you two, Kate?' Louise hesitated and when there was no answer went on, 'Robert's a very attractive man. Are you sure you're not overreacting to him because of that?'

It was a shrewd blow. Kate laughed scratchily. 'Oh, come on, Louise! You can't seriously think I'm languishing for him. I don't believe in that old love/hate theory. Robert Beaumont may be objective and impersonal in his judgments, but he's just too much of a cold fish for me. When he had Philip's picture in his hands, it just never occured to him that a person painted it and might be devastated by such a public dressing down. It would serve him right if Philip sued him.'

Louise shook her head. 'Yes, Robert was wrong there—I told him as much. Is it Philip's hurt pride that bothers you most about all this?'

His hurt pride and her own split feelings where Robert was concerned. Kate admitted privately that it was the latter that caused her most agitation.

'That and the arrogant way Beaumont has about him. I suppose he reminds me of Monte in some ways,' she muttered, 'And you know that I never liked Mum's husband.'

She could never call him a stepfather—always 'Mum's husband'. Louise nodded and accepted that readily. She was not partial to Monte Malvern either. He was arrogant and a first-class snob, which suited Kate's mother to perfection but which made him less than popular with Kate and Louise. It was a relief to them both that Monte's legal practice kept him and Fiona based in Victoria. Their only visits to Brisbane had been extraordinarily uncomfortable affairs, not to mention boring—as both Monte and Fiona tabled their successes, their influential friends, the exploits of Monte's children by his first marriage.

'I see. That explains a great deal. But I think you're wrong, Kate. Try and avoid the comparison. It's hardly fair to conduct a feud on the basis that the person reminds you of someone else.'

Kate was unable to promise that. Where Robert was concerned she could never be sure just what she would say or do next. The uncomplicated existence she had anticipated with Louise in the tranquillity of the mountains was a goal far from her reach, Kate realised, as long as he was within striking distance—literally and metaphorically. But sooner or later she knew she would have to make her apologies for her behaviour at their last meeting.

It was a week before she saw him again, and her avowed words of apology remained in her throat. For one thing, he greeted her in the garden as if nothing unpleasant had ever occurred between them. His 'Good morning, Kate' was pleasant and almost—avuncular. That was surprise enough to make her momentarily silent. The fact that he was wearing a track suit and sweating made her almost forget this was the cool, suave Robert Beaumont at all.

'Did you run down here?' she asked incredulously as he mopped his face with a narrow towel that hung about his neck.

'That's right. And it's unkind to make it sound so impossible, Kate. I'm really quite fit.' He waited expectantly for a moment, his lips twitching, and added, 'For my age.'

She tugged off her gardening gloves and looked up the steep slope. 'Will you run back?'

'Yes.'

'Do you do this often?' She looked him over. He seemed different dressed in the casual stretch clothes— less formidable?

'Every day,' he confessed. 'Haven't you ever seen me labouring past your door in the early morning, Kate?'

'Every day?' She was impressed. How did he find the time—or the stamina?

'Every day, I swear. Sometimes as I've gasped on the road, I've been tempted to call in and ask for a drink. But then, I thought, Kate wouldn't welcome a thirsting stranger at her door first thing in the morning.'

She smiled at his gentle sarcasm, trying to hold on to that last image of him—with his anger banked down but somehow exuding confidence and power. But he had turned into yet another man who seemed altogether less disturbing, though her cheeks were a little warm and her heartbeat a mite unsteady as they always were when he was around.

'No. You wouldn't be welcome,' she told him, and he was suddenly still. 'I'm not very sociable before breakfast.' A pause. 'Or during, for that matter.'

He looked hard at her and Kate became aware of her

wisping hair and the dirt on her arms. Probably her face was smeared too.

'I thought I'd be unwelcome for any other reason than that,' he murmured, and Kate's tardy defences went up in a rush.

'You caught me in a mellow mood, Mr Beaumont. It probably won't happen again.'

He sighed in mock regret. 'It was nice while it lasted.' Looking around at the rock garden Kate had laboured over, he walked away towards the house. 'Perhaps Louise will give me a drink. Will you join us, Kate?'

'I need no invitation from *you* to take refreshment in my own house,' she said sharply.

'While it lasted . . .' he repeated in a melancholy tone, then: 'Be careful with those bedding begonias, Kate. We sometimes get a late winter frost up here.' He walked away and ran lightly up the steps to knock once then enter.

'Know-it-all!' Kate muttered, and turned to look at the exuberant plants. What did he know about gardening, for heaven's sake? She was disgruntled by his appearance—and suspicious. It didn't seem possible that he could have put last Friday night from his mind—he had as good as warned her that he intended to make her sorry about that. She shoved her hands into the gloves again and crouched to dig the earth with a small fork. Her uneasiness grew. If his behaviour this morning was deliberately designed to push her off balance it had succeeded. But why was he being so pleasant?

The only answers were ones she didn't want to accept, or couldn't, and she worked doggedly at the weeds, burning to know what Robert and Louise were talking about and thirsting for a drink. But she was determined not to go in until he had left. So when Andrew's car crunched on to the drive she was there to help him settle Philip into his wheelchair.

'Kate, I know you're not officially open,' Philip grinned, 'but I'm hoping you'll let me in to buy something anyway.'

She laughed. 'You said the magic word, Philip— "Buy"! That's an Open Sesame around here, but . . .' she glanced at the house, 'Robert Beaumont's inside. Would you rather wait until he leaves?'

Philip's thin hands clenched on his knees. 'Never mind, Kate. Let's go in anyway.'

'What's he doing here?' Andrew demanded.

'He jogged down and went in to talk to Louise. It's a change to see him running instead of sweeping past in that expensive car of his.'

'I heard he was a fitness freak. 'Andrew sounded a bit sour and Kate knew he was thinking of Clarry's party when Robert had danced with her so intimately. He had glowered afterwards until Kate put a stop to his questions by melting in his arms. But she'd done that more in reaction to Robert than anything else and had regretted it ever since.

'He's something of a sportsman, I believe,' said Philip. 'He filled in for the school's coach last year.'

'Coach?' she queried.

'Football,' said Andrew as he manoeuvred the wheelchair to the stairs, then lifted his father out. Kate shook her head and took the chair, wondering if they were talking about the same man. Louise and Robert emerged from the kitchen just as Andrew settled his father in the wheelchair again.

Damn, Kate thought. What rotten luck that Robert should be here! Introductions were inevitable, and he would guess why she had suspended her usual judgment where Philip's painting was concerned. If he said anything to make the old man feel pitied she would hit him again.

Contrarily, when he did nothing of the sort, she was

furious with him anyway. His eyes met Kate's fleetingly when Philip was introduced and she saw his instant comprehension. To Philip he offered an apology of sorts. Shaking the old man's hand, he smiled, 'I imagine I'm not your favourite person right now. Was the truth too painful?'

Philip considered this opening with interest. 'The truth is always painful, Mr Beaumont. As I've no doubt you already know. I'm told you always tell the truth even about famous painters—so I guess I should be honoured to be treated the same. But I haven't quite convinced myself of that yet.'

Kate was fully expecting Robert to leave, but instead he lingered on, sitting down again with them while their visitors enjoyed a cup of tea. Anyone else would have departed from sheer embarrassment, she brooded. Instead he explained quite frankly to Philip how he felt about amateurs making profit from their hobby, and such was his charm that Philip seemed to accept it. In fact the old man was soon bandying words with him in equal frankness and obviously enjoying it.

Andrew was a different matter, however, his resentment of Robert remaining moodily on his handsome face. At least she had one ally, Kate thought, but it wasn't much consolation considering his reason was misplaced jealousy.

'I didn't like the way he was holding you, Kate,' he had said at Clarry's party, and she had squashed her annoyance at his possessive tone to agree, 'Neither did I.'

Now, he took her hand in full view of everyone and a little too loudly invited her to dinner with him and Philip. A little too enthusiastically, Kate agreed, and saw Robert's eyes on their clasped hands where they lay on the table top. For some reason he smiled as if enjoying some secret joke at their expense, and Kate's lips compressed. 'Don't let us keep you Mr Beaumont. You must be keen to get on with your running.'

'A short break is always welcome, Kate. That uphill climb isn't easy.'

'*Do* be careful, won't you?' she pleaded. 'Such stress can be dangerous in—older men.'

Robert grinned, showing white teeth and looking amazingly attractive with his hair damp and tousled from his towelling. 'Worried about my heart, Kate?'

Her own heart was thundering again, to her chagrin.

'Heart? Heavens, no! A heart attack is one thing I'm sure *you* don't need to worry about!'

But he merely chuckled to her annoyance. Louise shook her head and cast a warning glance at Kate, then took Philip into the gallery to look for the wedding present he needed for his niece.

Which left Kate making up an uneasy threesome with the two younger men. By the time Philip had chosen a set of goblets and pitcher for his niece, Kate was furious with Robert's complacency and heartily sick of Andrew's truculence. When the Barretts had left, she ignored Robert and went outside again. This time she retreated to the lean-to at the back so that she would not see him again as he departed.

But after a few minutes he followed her, and his broad-shouldered figure filled the doorway of the tiny space devoted to garden tools.

'What is it now, Mr Beaumont?' she asked testily to hide the jump of awareness that shook her. She was suddenly claustrophobic in the tiny room with him blocking her exit and most of the light.

'Just as I think I have you tabbed, you show me another Kate,' he said.

'What are you talking about? I don't show you anything.'

'Not willingly you don't.' She couldn't see his

expression because his head was silhouetted against the gold light of the day. After a moment he said: 'Let's forget your—impetuous bet about Philip's picture, shall we, Kate? In the circumstances it isn't quite fair.'

Hands on hips, she strained to see his face. 'I don't cry off, Mr Beaumont.'

'For God's sake, let's forget it.' The note of asperity in his voice reassured her. That was better, far better than his persuasive pleasantries. 'I can see now that you used no artistic measure of his work. You took it because you are what you are, Kate—and if I'd known I wouldn't have used his painting as I did.'

'And what am I, clever Mr Beaumont?'

'Most of the time you're a bad-tempered little——' he took a deep breath. 'But you're soft-hearted too, and that's why you took his work.'

'So I'm a rotten businesswoman. I couldn't give a damn what you think. But I stand by my word. The bet stays on.'

He came into the shed and Kate's senses sharpened. 'I don't know why I bother,' he muttered.

'Well, don't. I can live without you as a friendly neighbour!'

He laughed suddenly and she felt a stab of alarm. 'A friendly neighbour! Is that what you think I'm aiming to be?'

Kate stepped back unwarily and caught her foot on the mower. Her teeterings for balance were halted as Robert hitched an arm about her waist. She was stable again, yet teetering inside as if on a boat in troubled waters. Her hands rested on his chest, and as she tried to snatch them away, he drew her closer, trapping them against his damp warmth.

'Your boyfriend looked a bit put out today. Does he think he's playing second fiddle to Vincent—or someone else?' His teeth flashed white in the dimness, and Kate's colour rose at the reminder of her foolish ravings.

'Andrew knows he's number one as far as I'm concerned,' she snapped, and tried to wrench away from him.

'He was certainly laying claim rather obviously—your passionate responses to him at Clarry's place must have encouraged him.'

Kate pushed at his chest, dismayed that he had so accurately read her moves that night.

'Well, that's fine by me,' she assured him through gritted teeth. 'Andrew and I are very—compatible.' And make what you like of that, she thought.

'Are you?' He urged her closer and she strained away from him, pressing back against the mower handle until it hurt.

'Let me go Mr Beaumont! I'm not too fond of your brutish techniques.'

It was difficult to tell, but she thought his colour rose at the thrust. He spoke angrily enough to convince her that she had touched a sore spot.

'You've a harsh tongue, Kate. Does young Barrett bring out the softness in you? Do you show him the clinging, feminine side of yourself?'

'Don't be stupid! I'm neither clinging or soft.' But the words snapped out with more vehemence than was necessary as her body reacted to the sheer masculine feel of him—to the reined-in strength that held her there so effortlessly.

He laughed wryly. 'Yes, I could be wrong. But I swear I saw another Kate the first time we met. Those green eyes,' he stared down into them, suddenly serious, 'were wide and vulnerable and full of sweet surprise as if you'd——' he stopped, and Kate swallowed, her efforts to get away dwindling, her throat suddenly dry. In the close, dim gardening shed she was falling victim to the magic that had held her before. The touch of his mouth on hers was part of the spell, and slavishly she obeyed the impulses he dictated. Conscious thought ceased. It was instinct that spread her fingers across his chest and made her pliant beneath his questing hands. Her lips parted and the taste of him was as potent as the other sensations holding her there yielding in his arms.

Even when his kiss ended, she stayed, bemused, her body leaning on his in quiet intimacy, hearing and feeling the pound of his heartbeat, the shift of his chest as he breathed. For seconds she was content to remain, forgetting everything but the moment and the man. But she opened her eyes and was blinded by the golden glare from the doorway, and reality stiffened her body and washed painfully back into her brain. Robert's hands acknowledged her return to the defensive, by tightening to hold her there a moment longer.

'Does Barrett get that kind of response from you, Kate?' he asked softly, and she heard a note of elation in his voice. Or triumph.

Abruptly she pulled back, and he let her go. The mower handle scraped her thigh, but she scarcely felt it.

'Would you like me to allot you points on a scale of ten, Mr Beaumont?'

'Kate——'

'You're really rather good. But when I said I wasn't fond of your brutish methods, I wasn't asking for a demonstration of your alternative expertise!'

'Whether you asked or not, you participated willingly.'

She looked down. There was no denying that. Silently she cursed her weakness and reviewed her response to him with dismay.

She shrugged. 'It was rather novel, I suppose. Being

kissed in the garden shed was something I'd never experienced.'

'Let me know if there are any more gaps in your experience, Kate,' he grinned. 'I'll be glad to oblige.'

'You're never obliging, Mr Beaumont. And I shall apply to Andrew if I require any similar enlightenment. Kindly keep your necking for your girl-friend in future.'

'Necking . . .?' He pressed his mouth into a thin line and took a deep breath. 'One of these days, Kate, you'll go too far and I'll put you over my knee for a hiding you won't forget!'

The wish to hit him clenched her fists, but she resisted, remembering the last time. She had no desire to be back in his arms so soon after losing herself in them.

'You won't tempt me with your kinky threats. If that's the sort of thing you fancy, you'd better . . .' She saw the blaze in his eyes and backed away, fouling the lawn mower again and falling painfully across its hard metal bulk. This time he made no attempt to save her but contemplated her sprawling figure with frustrated fury squaring his shoulders.

'If I ever do it, Kate, you won't find it a bit kinky. But think of me tonight when you see the bruises on your beautiful behind.'

She stopped rubbing the hurt of the mower's several projections. 'If you hadn't collected them from the mower I might have applied them myself!'

Then he was gone, and the doorway threw its brilliant rectangle of light across the cluttered shed.

That night in the bathroom, Kate stared at her naked body in the mirror and remembered his words. The bruises had appeared, dark and angry on the soft, pale skin, and she viewed them with a strange sense of repulsion, as if he *had* put them there. But as she quickly drew on a nightdress to cover herself, she admitted that it wasn't this kind of bruising she feared from Robert Beaumont.

CHAPTER FIVE

IT was a while before she had to speak to him again. With a cunning she hadn't known she possessed, she managed to be either leaving the house or just returning, so that his arrivals and departures occasioned only the merest nod of the head and maybe a reluctant 'Hello' if Louise was present. Robert, on the other hand, was as charming as ever, and she was aware that his courteous behaviour made her look increasingly ungracious in comparison.

She saw him one morning, jogging up the road and went to the car, wishing she had gone a little earlier for the newspaper that she often fetched to read over breakfast. He detoured from the road and came over as she started the engine. With nonchalant assurance he leaned on the window edge and looked in at her, his breathing heavy but regular. In her working clothes and with her hair wildly loose having had a brush barely dragged through it, Kate wondered what made his inspection of her so thorough. As his eyes roved her make-up-free face she in turn noticed the glowing health of him. His grey eyes were clear and his skin a natural summer tan. The broad muscularity of his shoulders filled the window, and Kate was anxious to be away from his overwhelming aura of power.

'Flagging, Mr Beaumont?' she enquired as he continued to rest there, saying nothing.

His gaze wandered again over her face, lingering on her mouth. 'I believe I am, Kate.'

'Maybe you'll have to find a short cut if the long climb home is proving too much for you.'

'A short cut,' he murmured, watching her with an odd expression. 'Yes—I wish I could find one.'

'You could always cut through the tangle at the back of our land, but you might have trouble with snakes,' she offered with mock sincerity.

His smile was rueful. 'I'm afraid that's often the drawback with short cuts. They're fraught with dangers. I think I'll continue to take the long way around.' He stood up and watched her drive away. Kate put her foot down, curiously disturbed by the conversation which seemed so simple, yet assumed undertones because it was with Robert.

It became more difficult to avoid him, and Kate gave up after a time because the effort affected her work at the gallery. Inevitably he tossed the occasional sceptical comment at her about the work she hung in the gallery, and eventually she realised that he was merely baiting her for a response. So she kept her replies light, careless as if she didn't care what he thought, although deep down she made the sobering admission that she was beginning to wish for his approval.

'By the way, Mr Beaumont,' she said to him once, 'that Parisian scene that you were so scathing about was sold yesterday.'

He grinned. 'Does that prove something, Kate? Other than that your buyer was uninformed and a bit hasty. He paid a high price for a worthless picture.'

'He liked it—therefore the price wasn't too high. Of course, I was painfully honest with him—told him it wasn't genuine art, pointed out that the artist wasn't a name—but he wanted it anyway. Seemed quite relieved that he wouldn't need to install a burglar alarm to protect it against art thieves.'

To her annoyance he just laughed and refused to further the argument, but that, she thought later, was probably because Louise was present. And Robert saved his very best behaviour for when her aunt was there. When they were alone . . . Kate reddened at the recollection of their private clashes and her own foolish reaction during the last one. She vowed to ensure that she did not repeat her folly.

And she didn't. But instead of being pleased about it, she grew more restless than ever, more ill at ease when Robert was about and it became a strain to lightly dismiss his remarks both personal and about her modest collection of paintings. Kate's confidence had dwindled as Louise's pottery sales steadily increased and the picture gallery limped along. Only the knowledge of Robert's 'Highly Commended' enabled her to combat the teasing comments that nevertheless held his unchanging criticism of her judgment. His derogatory statements about her gallery didn't, however, extend to the craft section. Robert openly admired Louise's work and promptly purchased the newest of her superb fantasy items.

It was a water jug of classic shape and proportion, naiads with long, flowing hair and slender limbs forming the handle and poised on the false rim where a perpetual pool of water gleamed blue. She had used glass which melted in the firing in a delicate operation to produce the tranquil strip of liquid. The moment Robert set eyes on it he announced his intention to buy it.

The money would go a long way to covering several bills that had come in, and Kate was glad of it. But as she watched him turn the lovely object in his strong, shapely hands a pang of jealousy shot through her, that her aunt could always earn his approval while she . . . she could only do so under an alias. The thought annoyed so much that she turned on her heel and left the gallery, only to be found in the garden by Robert before he left with the wrapped jug.

He looked at her coppery hair, which was twisted carelessly into a roll at the back.

'Louise tells me you're twenty-two. Isn't it time you conquered your childish pettishness? A little pleasure in your aunt's sale would be considered normal instead of your jealous reaction.'

Kate's face flamed as red as her hair. That he had detected her flash of envy was bad enough. She could only hope that he didn't guess the real reason which had made her forget temporarily her pleasure for Louise. Naturally she would be jubilant with her over the sale—of course she would congratulate her. She of all people was Louise's stoutest supporter. But she knew she had let her own feelings make her flounce off and felt guilty. To have him standing there delivering her a lecture on something she knew only too well was unbearable. She wondered, too, what else Louise had told him, apart from her age.

He had found her at the side of the house where she had fled to pick up tools in an effort to convert her feelings into energy. Watching her with the shadows of an Indian hawthorn dancing across his face, he looked more ruggedly attractive in the casual cords and sweater. His dark hair was a little shaggier than when she had first seen him, and Kate found time in her fury to reflect that he looked compelling either way. The knowledge made her snatch a pair of shears from the ground. Her elbows jerked as she snipped at the lower straggling branches of the hawthorn.

'Don't lecture me, Mr Beaumont. I'm fully aware of my family obligations and Louise understands me very well.'

He followed the sharp movements of the shears as twigs and leaves fell to the ground.

'Yes, I think she does. It's a pity you haven't a grain of understanding of yourself.'

Kate turned to him, face hot and high in colour, the shears splayed in her hands. 'Oh, and what makes you think that?'

His smile flashed, showing white, even teeth. The crinkles about his eyes deepened. She willed herself to break eye contact and snapped at a dry twig with vigour. It shot sideways on to the grass.

'For instance,' he went on, 'you probably think all this activity is trimming your garden.'

The clippers squeaked as she tore into the mass of branches and browned old flower heads. 'Exactly what it is doing!'

'No, Kate,' he grinned, his eyes on the flashing secateurs, 'you're not cutting that tree. You're cutting me down to size. But I warn you, it's not that easy.'

He walked away as he said it, down the side of the house where his car was parked.

'Goodbye, Dr Freud,' she called after him. 'Don't hurry back!'

But above the frantic sounds of her clipping she heard only a deep chuckle.

Louise worked placidly on, filling the orders that Max procured for her from the Gold Coast speciality shops and spending much of her free time with him. She had grown to like Robert a lot, apparently, and had put his past criticisms from her mind. Kate found herself continually biting her tongue when Louise brought his name quite naturally into their conversations, and finding excuses to avoid the cosy little tea breaks that occurred when Robert dropped in.

And the more he was around, the more things seemed to go wrong. The hot water system burnt out its element and the stove refused to heat. Kate spent the sale money from her painting on repairs and muttered nasty things about Robert under her breath, as if he was in some way responsible for the breakdowns.

Evan Gale sent her a catalogue of paintings he would show with them, the numbers reduced owing to unexpected sales and not sufficient, Kate felt, for a one-man show, which presented her with another problem. She decided she needed another painter's work as well and asked Max for a list of the C.A.G.'s members. Among them she would surely find someone with ten decent pictures to exhibit, and if not she would have to put her own collection with Evan's. All signed 'Ransome', of course. That at least Beaumont did not know about and couldn't spoil. He certainly had made an impact everywhere else, Kate thought gloomily.

When she went out to tend her rock garden one morning and found the begonias browned and miserable, she felt as if he had somehow jinxed them. He appeared to be determined to become part of their lives and Kate was equally determined to remain out of his reach. But she was contrarily irked when he appeared to give up on her, concentrating on Louise when he called and sparing her only the casual greeting or farewell that she preferred. It should have pleased her, but instead she found the irritating man as strong a presence as ever.

Even the dinner with Philip and Andrew Barrett was not quite free of Beaumont overtones, with Philip inclined to like Robert after their meeting and Andrew struggling to say anything civil at all about him. Kate kept her responses light, breezy, hoping to undo the impression she had given Andrew lately, aware that Robert was subtly intruding even as she chose her words.

But overall the evening was an enjoyable one. Philip Barrett presided over the table, his thin face flushed with pleasure at Kate's response to his 'tall tales', as Andrew called his recollections of his youth. But as the meal ended, his conversation dwindled into breathlessness and Kate was reminded that it was not paralysis that confined him to a wheelchair but his crippled lungs.

'It's time for the invalid to retire, Kate.' He gallantly kissed her hand before he went with Andrew in attendance.

'How about coffee and a brandy, Kate?' Andrew's blue eyes were definitely romantic when he came back and turned off the main living room lights to switch on a shaded lamp.

'Not until we've cleared away,' she said briskly, and insisted on removing the table settings, then rolled up the sleeves of her silk blouse to wash up.

'Kate, leave that.' Andrew slid his arms about her from behind and nuzzled her neck. 'We've got better things to do than housework.'

'Don't be silly—as if I'd leave you with all this work!' She whisked up a lather in the sink and froth flew.

Andrew wiped some off his hands as he sighed and moved away from her.

'You're just too good to be true—do you know that, Kate?' He fetched a towel and began to wipe dishes, smiling at her in undiminished warmth.

'Not me. I have it on good authority that I'm bad-tempered and stubborn.'

'Who would say a thing like that?' he grinned, then sobered. 'Beaumont—he's the only one who would talk to you like that.' His good humour paled and he mulled over it for a few seconds. 'I think he fancies you.'

Kate bent over a saucepan and scrubbed for all she was worth. 'What makes you think that?'

'Just the way he looks at you—the way he was holding you at Clarry's party. But don't let him get to you, Kate. He's as good as engaged to Sonia Marsden, but she's such a cool one that he might want a fling on the side. That's all it would be, Kate,' he told her earnestly.

The saucepan clattered to the sink. 'Look, Andrew—don't warn me about him. It just isn't necessary because *I* don't fancy him. Anyway,' she went on, her green eyes angry, 'you're not my keeper.'

She wiped down the surfaces with unnecessary energy, but found the cloth removed from her hand by an unexpectedly dominating Andrew. He was smiling again, pleased at her avowal of uninterest in Beaumont, and pulled her close to whisper. 'I might like that job, Kate.' Just for a moment she let herself relax against him. She was quite abruptly weary of fighting and tension. Lately even Louise's closeness was denied her—her friendship with Robert and her growing regard for Max making an outsider of Kate. Andrew was nice, his arms were strong and warm around her. She closed her eyes and wished it was like this with ... she drew back hastily from the unbidden thoughts of just how it *had* been with Robert, and reminded herself that it was this kind of stupidity that had given Andrew the wrong idea in the beginning.

'I'll bet you say that to all the girls, Andrew,' she teased. 'Like, for instance, that sweet brunette who found you so entertaining at the art show.'

'Rachel? That's different. We went out a few times, but . . .' he grinned. 'You're jealous, Kate.'

She denied it, groaning inwardly that she had only made things worse. Damn Robert Beaumont! It was all his fault.

They had the coffee seated in the lounge—Andrew looking very pleased with himself and Kate shooting glances at her watch and dropping hints that she couldn't stay late.

'I could have picked you up and taken you home,' Andrew said. 'Why did you insist on driving over yourself?'

'I like to be independent, Andrew.'

'Yes, you're that all right. But you haven't lost any femininity along the way like some women. You, Kate,' he put his arms about her and spoke with his mouth against her hair, 'are a woman—a true woman who needs a man.'

But you're not the one, she thought, wishing he could be. It would be so simple with Andrew.

'Kate, I'm going to the coast for the weekend soon. Will you come with me?'

She was unable to think of anything to say to that. Not because she was shocked—she wasn't. To go away with a man would not offend her, if it was the right man and she felt committed. But so far there hadn't been a right man, and Andrew wasn't the one.

'But what about your father?' she said, ridiculously, and the question seemed to give Andrew hope.

'The nurse will come in. How about it, Kate?' He caressed her, kissed her, and Kate wished his touch was exciting enough to make the answer 'yes'. What was the matter with her, that a man she liked so much could fail to arouse her yet another whom she almost hated had only to walk into the room to warm her skin and raise her pulse rate?

'I don't think so, Andrew.' She put up a hand to his face and smiled at him so sadly that he drew back.

'I must go,' she announced into the moody silence, and he went with her to her car.

'It's him, I suppose,' Andrew blurted at last, and Kate pretended bewilderment.

'Beaumont—that's why you've cooled to me. How could you, Kate, when he's treated you as he has?'

'You're wrong, Andrew. Robert Beaumont is everything I can't stand. I had enough of his kind of attitudes from my own mother. She made my father's life a misery because of her snobbish ways, then left him and married a man who's a mirror image of Beaumont—and I can't stand him either.'

Who am I kidding? she thought as Andrew took her hand and pressed it.

'In that case, I won't give up yet.'

Kate drove away with the feeling that they were both clutching at straws. Later still, she wondered if it was true that Robert and Sonia Marsden were deeply involved. Somehow even though they made an attractive couple, Kate found it difficult to imagine them married. But Sonia herself supplied confirmation to that. She turned up at the gallery looking about with lofty distaste at the paintings and at Kate.

'Robert said you had some decent pottery,' she said in a voice of total uninterest. 'I won't tell you what he said about your pictures.'

Kate managed a smile for this girl who gave her a most uncivilised urge to scratch. Her eyes dropped to Sonia's long-tipped fingers—the girl outmatched her there. Then she met Sonia's cool, smug gaze. And there too, Kate thought. She turned to lead the way to the pottery with a vision of Sonia's blonde beauty held close in Robert's arms. There was no doubt they looked good together. And they probably deserved each other.

'You don't need to be tactful, Miss Marsden.' Which was somewhat tongue-in-cheek considering the girl's blatant lack of it, 'Mr Beaumont tells me what he thinks of them every time he comes here.' The girl's gaze sharpened and Kate reflected that it had been the wrong thing to say. But surely this poised woman wouldn't feel threatened by her?

Sonia Marsden took her time browsing among the more expensive lines that were displayed with Louise's customary flair.

'Mmmm, I like it,' she said at last, as if she'd not

been expecting to. 'I was afraid it might be as amateurish as the pictures.'

Kate's temper stirred. 'Surely not—if Robert recommended it.' She accompanied the words with a big smile, but Sonia wasn't fooled. Her mouth pouted a bit as she lifted the lid off a massive casserole dish and her eyes weren't at all apologetic when she almost dropped it. 'Oh, dear, I nearly dropped it,' she said, and Kate felt like pushing her out of the door.

'Yes, you nearly did, didn't you?'

'This is nice,' the girl pointed. 'I'm looking for a wedding present for a friend, but the trouble is, every time I shop for someone else I see the things I want for my own wedding presents. Silly, isn't it?'

Kate moved her mouth in an automatic smile. 'Yes, it is,' she agreed.

'This, for instance.' Sonia's red nails clicked as she ran her fingers down the generous curves of a metre-high jar. 'This would look lovely in the foyer—have you seen Robert's foyer?' Then she laughed. 'Of course you haven't. But this would look super in it.'

After a while she bought the big casserole dish and waved a languid hand at the jar as she went. 'Yes, I rather fancy that. I must tell Robert to call in and see what he thinks of it.'

Kate saw her to the door. 'Don't drop it now, Miss Marsden,' she said bitchily as the girl stumbled on the stairs and tightened her hold on the package. 'We don't do refunds.'

So, Kate thought as she fetched another dish to fill the vacancy on the shelves, Andrew was right about those two. She wiped the dust off the new piece with such a brisk hand that it almost fell to the floor. The day was full of potential accidents, she thought dryly, re-membering Sonia's spiteful feigned clumsiness. The girl

really disliked her, which wasn't surprising, she
supposed. Her nasty rejoinder at Clarry's place hadn't
exactly been designed to inculcate friendship. But her
feelings about the blonde girl today bothered Kate. She
wasn't normally so catty. And afterwards she asked
herself just why Sonia Marsden's visit should have
depressed her so much. But she couldn't come up with a
sensible answer.

In fact, Kate thought moodily, she seemed to be
rather short on answers lately. Plenty of questions but
no solutions. What to do about Andrew, for instance.
Reluctant to give him a flat 'no', she agreed to have
dinner with him at the coast, hoping to ease out of the
relationship slowly. They went to a dimly lit restaurant
in Surfers' Paradise, with moody music and fine food
that they tasted but barely saw. They talked and danced
and drank champagne to celebrate the sale of one of
Andrew's watercolours.

'It's as much my celebration as yours, Andrew,' she
told him. 'I badly need a few sales to bolster my ego.
Louise's pottery is going hand over fist—and besides,
I'd like to prove to——'

'Beaumont?' he supplied dryly. 'He's really got under
your skin, hasn't he?'

'More like a burr under a sock, actually. The more
you stamp on it, the more it irritates.' Andrew was right
the first time, she admitted silently. 'Under her skin'
was rather more apt.

They danced again.

'I hope I didn't offend you, Kate, when I asked you
to come away with me. It's not that I think—um—that
you're——'

Kate laughed. 'A scarlet woman? It's okay, Andrew.
You didn't offend me at all.'

'Will you reconsider—a bit later, perhaps? Maybe I
rushed you a bit, but I thought——'

She knew what he thought. Guiltily she admitted the blame for much of what he thought. 'I'm very fond of you, Andrew.'

'Boy,' he said ruefully, 'you certainly know how to dampen a man's ego!'

'What's wrong with "fond"?' she smiled at him, trying to keep it light, and he played along, recognising his only chance.

'Nothing, I guess. It makes me sound a bit like your pet pekingese, though.'

Kate's laugh rang out. 'Not a pekingese, Andrew—definitely not that.'

'What, then?' he prompted, and she knew she couldn't tell him he was like a brother—it wasn't quite true anyway.

'Fond—as in cousins,' she offered, and he sighed and held her close as the music picked up tempo.

'Make it kissing cousins and I'll have to be content with that.'

She sidestepped his plans for another date quite simply. 'I can't make any plans for quite a few weeks. We've got this exhibition for Evan Gale coming up and I'll be terribly busy.'

He nodded and agreed to postpone their next date until after the show. When he kissed her goodnight, Kate still had no solution to the problem of Andrew, who was too nice to hurt and not right enough to love.

As she drifted on the edge of sleep that night, Kate found herself thinking of another problem. Unbidden the memory of a strangely magical few seconds came to mind. The seconds during which she had stood passively in Robert's arms after he had seduced her with a kiss that bore no resemblance to any other. And the trouble with this problem, she thought muzzily, closing her eyes, was that not only had she no answers—she didn't even know that the questions were.

CHAPTER SIX

Two mornings later Kate was frustratedly peering into the van's inactive motor. Maybe the battery terminals were loose, she thought, and tapped them experimentally with the spanner she had brought out on the offchance of finding something recognisably loose in the maze.

The darned car was working all right last night, she grumbled. It had toiled its way up the hill a little sluggishly, to be sure, as it always did and she had moved over to allow a gleaming white sports car to overtake. Robert had used the horn in mocking greeting as he passed with Sonia Marsden in the passenger seat beside him.

'Damn!' she exclaimed as the spanner slipped and her knuckle hit cold metal. She wondered if Sonia had come back down the mountain yet. Andrew might label her 'cool', but Kate didn't believe she would stay that way if Robert decided otherwise. She had reason to believe that his powers of persuasion were highly developed—and Sonia Marsden would be a great deal more receptive to them than she herself had been. 'Double damn!' She straightened and put her knuckles to her mouth. As she did, she saw Robert come into view in his jogging clothes.

'Speak of the devil!' she muttered.

He slowed his pace and turned into the drive, his tall body taut and lithe in the track suit.

'What a plaintive figure you make, Kate—all alone with a car that's obviously not working!' He pulled up close to her, his chest heaving a little and a fine mist on his forehead. With one hand he unzipped his jacket and pushed it back to set his hands on his hips while he looked her over with some amusement. In her jeans and tee-shirt with grease liberally spattered about, probably on her face too, Kate knew she wasn't looking her best. He had a talent for catching her at the wrong time. Then again—anytime was the wrong time where he was concerned.

'And you, Mr Beaumont—running all alone! Where's your friend?' She bit her tongue, but it was too late. He knew she was thinking of his blonde passenger of the night before.

'If you mean Sonia, I'd say she's still in bed.'

But whose bed? Kate thought as her mind threw up a series of vivid pictures for her. 'You'll want to be going, then,' she said rudely. 'Please don't feel any need to stop and exchange courtesies with me, Mr Beaumont.'

'Exchange?' he mocked, and put out a hand to lean his weight on the car. Lazily he crossed one leg in front of the other, the picture of a man who had no intention of leaving.

'When do you ever do any work?' she snapped, and turned her attention to the car's engine again.

'I'm working all the time, Kate. Working to acquaint the world with "genuine art", working to keep fit—

working to get what I want.' He too leaned under the bonnet and Kate met his eyes briefly above the gaskets and spark plugs and hoses.

'You must have everything you want already, surely?'

'Not everything. I see your trouble—give me the spanner.'

'Where is it? I can fix it if you show me where,' she said obstinately.

A large hand closed over hers and his other plucked the spanner from her grasp. Kate withdrew, red-faced and furious at his show of strength. In a moment he too stood up, flicked a hard look at her and went to try the ignition. Almost she wished it wouldn't start, though she badly needed the van this morning. But of course it did.

He returned the spanner to her. 'And now I suppose you're going to embarrass me with effusive thanks.' She tried to summon up the words, but stayed silent.

'No? Well then, I'm not too proud to take what's not offered.' Before she could move he snapped his arms about her and kissed her, warmly and urgently, taking advantage of her surprise to make more than a mere token of it. Kate's hands, spanner and all, were curved to his muscular back and seeking to explore further before she recovered. When her struggles failed to release her she pressed the spanner hard and he grunted, then let her go.

'You—you're a—a——' she started, and tossed back her ruffled hair.

'Blame yourself, Kate. A simple thank you would have saved you all that agony. Although,' he stared at her flushed cheeks, 'you seemed to like it at first.'

Kate fumed as she returned his look. She *did* have grease on her face—for now he was wearing a black streak near his mouth too. 'You've got grease on your mouth,' she told him coldly. 'You'd better come in and wash up.'

As they went to the stairs he said conversationally, 'I see the begonias didn't survive the frost last week,' and laughed softly at Kate's darkling glance.

Louise seemed surprised to see them come in together.

'Sorry, Louise, no newspaper today. The car wouldn't start. But Mr Beaumont found the trouble.'

'I even managed to fix this trouble,' he smiled, 'I'm not always so fortunate.'

Louise thanked him and cast thoughtful eyes on the matching grease marks.

'You can use the bathroom first, Mr Beaumont, as you're the hero of the day,' Kate said waspishly, and was pleased to see that he was annoyed.

'How gracious of you, Kate.'

After her turn in the bathroom, Kate went to the kitchen to find Robert enjoying not just coffee, but breakfast with them.

'What's this—comb honey?' he asked Louise when she put a pottery jar on the table.

'Even better—wild honey. One of Max's customers brought it into the shop. He's always bringing us his leftover produce. Try some—it's delicious.'

He sampled it and agreed. 'I haven't tasted wild honey for years,' he said, and looked at Kate. 'I came across some not long ago in a place renowned for it— but it turned out to be sour.'

A place renowned for it ... Kate spread her toast briskly. He was harking back to Mount Coot-tha again and that first stupid meeting.

'Surely honey doesn't sour?' Louise echoed, frowning as she picked up the vibrations between them.

'Certain kinds do. But the process is reversible, I believe, if it's caught in time.'

For the life of her Kate couldn't think of a thing to say. What exactly did all this double-talk mean? Did he imagine that he would wear her down until she became a meek little doormat, accepting all his criticisms as an uninformed woman should?

'At any rate, this is delicious,' Robert beamed at Louise. 'I needed something strong to take the taste of grease away—can't think how I got it in my mouth.'

Louise cast him an old-fashioned look, but he merely held out his cup for more coffee. 'Are you free tomorrow, Kate?' he enquired, and her head came up warily.

'Why?'

'The bet you made—the first one. You haven't sold the painting within six weeks. Time to pay up, Kate.'

She recognised the words he had used to her that night—the night he had made love to her at her invitation. The tell-tale colour rushed to her cheeks as she recalled her reactions to him—not all feigned—and the wanton way she had lured him on only to repulse him. Robert watched and waited until she looked up again and she knew he had used the phrase on purpose to evoke memories of that night she would prefer to forget. And there were several episodes she would prefer to forget since then too.

'Tomorrow,' he said again, 'and tomorrow night. You'll work for me in the afternoon and have dinner with me in the evening.'

'That just might not suit me, Mr Beaumont—as it happens I have a few things planned for tomorrow and . . .'

'You said you wouldn't cry off, Kate.'

Louise sighed in exasperation. 'Look, this is childish. Robert, surely you aren't going to insist on this ridiculous bet being honoured? You've met Philip and you must realise why Kate accepted his work.'

'Exactly what I said to Kate. I offered to forget all about it, but she insisted that it stand.'

The look her aunt gave her relegated Kate to fourth grade again. She clicked her tongue and rose from the table. 'Then I'll leave you two to fight it out,' she said, and went through the curtained doorway into her studio.

Vincent shot under the curtain in an excess of energy as he chased a moth. The silence dragged out, broken only by the tiny sharp sounds of the kitten's claws on the timber floor. Kate rose and began to gather up the empty cups and plates.

'Tomorrow then, Kate,' Robert pressed.

'All right. But—about dinner afterwards—that's hardly necessary.'

He smiled. 'Nevertheless we'll have it. You agreed, if you remember.'

Yes, she had agreed, and insisted on keeping the arrangement when he would have let her off the hook. Not for the first time since meeting Robert, Kate bemoaned her hasty tongue.

'In that case, perhaps you'd be good enough to tell me what kind of clothes would be suitable for what you have in mind.'

'For what I have in mind?' He smiled wolfishly at her.

Kate blinked and felt a tremor of apprehension. There was no way out of this, and it was her own fault. But surely he couldn't seduce her in the rarified atmosphere of his gallery or in a restaurant. When she didn't answer he went on: 'Wear that silky outfit you had on at Clarry's party. Bring it with you. You can change at the gallery.'

'But I could come home first . . .'

'We'll be working *my* gallery hours, Kate. Tomorrow they're noon to six-thirty. I'd like to go directly to dinner when we finish.'

'Well,' she said a little petulantly, 'we must do it your way, of course . . .'

'Thank you, Kate. I'll see you at noon tomorrow.' He inclined his head mockingly and went to the door.

Kate realised that she hadn't offered her apology for that awful night yet and sighed in resignation. It would have to be tomorrow, and much as she hated the idea she would have to do it for her own self-respect. And that had been steadily plummeting ever since she had met Robert. She had begun lying and prevaricating, provoking anger and allowing herself to be provoked into ridiculous outbursts. In twenty-two years she had probably committed less folly than she had in the past few months. If only she hadn't made this crazy bet!

And by the time she was ready to leave for Beaumont Galleries before lunch the next day, she regretted it even more. For she was pondering on the irony of an unkind fate that had brought a buyer for Philip's painting a day too late. Not, of course, that it was all bad. She was pleased for Philip and looked forward to his pleasure in this genuine sale.

'If only she'd come in yesterday!' Kate exclaimed to Louise, who was driving the short distance to drop her off so that she would have the car for the day. Robert would, Kate assumed, bring her home after their dinner.

Louise snorted. 'It's a miracle anyone came in to buy that. I was amazed the first time, but I can hardly believe it this time.'

'Well,' Kate began with a hint of a laugh, 'Mrs Price did say she was looking for something to go with her curtains.'

As they drew near to Robert's place, Louise cleared her throat. 'Er—tonight, Kate, when you get home . . .' she was almost stammering, and Kate looked at her in surprise, 'I—er—I'm going down to Max's place and . . .'

LOVE BEYOND REASON
There was a surprise in store for Amy!

Amy had thought nothing could be as perfect as the days she had shared with Vic Hoyt in New York City—before he took off for his Peace Corps assignment in Kenya.

Impulsively, Amy decided to follow. She was shocked to find Vic established in his new life... and interested in a new girl friend.

Amy faced a choice: be smart and go home... or stay and fight for the only man she would ever love.

MAN OF POWER
Sara took her role seriously

Although Sara had already planned her escape from the subservient position in which her father's death had placed her, Morgan Haldane's timely appearance had definitely made it easier.

All Morgan had asked in return was that she pose as his fiancée. He'd confessed to needing protection from his partner's wife, Louise, and that part of Sara's job proved easy.

But unfortunately for Sara's heart, Morgan hadn't told her about Monique...

Your Romantic Adventure Starts Here.

THE LEO MAN
"He's every bit as sexy as his father!"

Her grandmother thought that description would appeal to Rowan, but Rowan was determined to avoid any friendship with the arrogant James Fraser.

Aboard his luxury yacht, that wasn't easy. When they were all shipwrecked on a tropical island, it proved impossible.

And besides, if it weren't for James, none of them would be alive. Rowan was confused. Was it merely gratitude that she now felt for this strong and rugged man?

THE WINDS OF WINTER
She'd had so much— now she had nothing

Anne didn't dwell on it, but the pain was still with her—the double-edged pain of grief and rejection.

It had greatly altered her; Anne barely resembled the girl who four years earlier had left her husband, David. He probably wouldn't even recognize her—especially with another name.

Anne made up her mind. She just *had* to go to his house to discover if what she suspected was true...

These FOUR free Harlequin Romance novels allow you to enter the world of romance, love and desire. As a member of the Harlequin Home Subscription Plan, you can continue to experience all the moods of love. You'll be inspired by moments so real...so moving...you won't want them to end. So start your own Harlequin Romance adventure by returning the reply card below. DO IT TODAY!

TAKE THESE 4 BOOKS AND TOTE BAG FREE!

Mail to: Harlequin Reader Service
2504 W. Southern Avenue, Tempe, AZ 85282

YES, please send me FREE and without obligation my 4 Harlequin Romances. If you do not hear from me after I have examined my 4 FREE books, please send me the 6 new Harlequin Romances each month as soon as they come off the presses. I understand that I will be billed only $9.00 for all 6 books. There are no shipping and handling nor any other hidden charges. There is no minimum number of books that I have to purchase. In fact, I can cancel this arrangement at any time. The first 4 books and the tote bag are mine to keep as FREE gifts, even if I do not buy any additional books.

116-CIR-EAUU

NAME _____ (please print) _____

ADDRESS _____ APT. NO. _____

CITY _____ STATE _____ ZIP _____

Signature (If under 18, parent or guardian must sign).

Comprehension dawned. 'You might stay the night, is that it?'

With heightened colour Louise nodded. The car turned into the elegant Beaumont drive edged with clipped shrubs and ground cover. 'Yes. Do you mind?'

'Mind? Why should I mind? And why would you care if I did, Louise darling? You're over twenty-one and can do whatever you like.'

Kate got out of the van and went around to take her evening clothes from the back where she had carefully laid them. Her small beauty case held her make-up and a larger bag carried her best shoes and a clutch purse.

''Bye, Louise. Have fun!' she smiled delightedly at the brick red face of her aunt, who seemed to be suffering almost adolescent embarrassment. She was still smiling when she stepped up on to the vine-draped patio of Beaumont Galleries.

Robert stood waiting and the delight ebbed from her face under his intent gaze.

'For one moment I thought that brilliant smile was for me,' he said mockingly, and Kate almost wished *this* was a new beginning. Her heartbeat skipped at the sight of him, tanned and powerful in an open-necked shirt and tweedy trousers and jacket. She put her head on one side, considering. 'Not for you, Mr Beaumont. But maybe for the thrill of entering your hallowed portals. At last, I thought to myself—I'm about to see some genuine art.'

He smiled at her sarcasm and took the small case from her, moving inside. They entered a narrow hall, starkly plain with a black and white ceramic floor and a piece of traditional sculpture on a marble stand. Kate followed him through to an office where he slid open a door to reveal some drawers and hanging space. A few items of his clothing were on hangers and Kate reached up to hang her dress next to them. It was a strangely intimate sight—her silky dress and jacket submissively draped next to a spare shirt and masculine dark blazer. She turned away abruptly and raised her eyes to him as he reached out to close the panel.

'His and hers,' he grinned, aggravatingly accurate.

Kate looked around the office, noticing the quietly expensive fittings and the superb low-key painting in its gilt frame. But her eyes fixed on the antique desk. Or more particularly on the silver ice bucket and bottle of wine that sat on its polished mahogany surface. And the sandwiches and assorted delicacies beside it. Two glasses and two plates clearly stated that this was lunch, and Kate looked at them with dismay. 'Work at my gallery for a day,' he had said, and she had imagined a quick tour of the gallery, then being tucked away somewhere to attend to his paperwork. Not this cosy atmosphere for two in his lushly appointed office. And, she remembered, where was his manager—Ben Strickland?

'I gave Ben the day off—as you were coming to assist me, Kate,' Robert told her blandly, and she hid her alarm that he could read her so surely. 'Just the two of us running a gallery together—who would believe it?' He made it sound so intimate—so permanent that she knew a twang of regret that he was only baiting her. But she returned to the offensive—or what had lately become the defensive.

'I daresay nobody would, seeing the very cosy lunch laid out here. I'm willing to work for you today, Mr Beaumont, but if you want to share champagne lunches with someone, phone your friend Sonia.'

Robert's good humour paled, his face hardened and she was glad to see the change. 'Louise tells me you aren't so rude to any other men, so it must be only me who merits your shrewish behaviour. Tell me why, Kate.'

She had asked herself the same question a hundred times and skirted around the answer. It was safer to face his annoyance with her than his admiration—she knew that. And sometimes in the dark of night she had even admitted to her vulnerability where he was concerned. It would be so easy to allow herself to fall under his spell—she had once and fortunately been saved by the revelation of his true self. Lately she had even begun to doubt that her assessment of that was correct, but even so, some ingrained caution made her cling to hostility. She shrugged her shoulders.

'The reason is obvious, I would have thought. And Louise isn't quite right. You are one of two men who bring out the worst in me.'

'Ah yes—your stepfather. Not quite the same thing.'

Kate began to speculate on what else they had discussed in their heart-to-hearts over coffee. She was angered that Louise had mentioned her at all to this man.

'Almost exactly the same thing. *He's* an arrogant snob too.'

'I'm not——' he began, then turned away to open the wine. As it gurgled into the glasses he glanced at her. 'Why did your mother marry an arrogant snob, Kate?'

'Because like attracts like. Does that shock you, Mr Beaumont? That I should criticise my own mother?'

He expelled a breath in a grunt of laughter. 'Nothing you could say would shock me any more, Kate. Tell me what this other snob does for a living.'

She grasped the wineglass and wished she had never embarked on the subject. 'I daresay you may even know him. He's a barrister practising in Melbourne—Monte Malvern.'

His brows shot up. 'I know of him. He's much in demand legally and socially, from what I gather. How does your mother fit into that scene?'

'Perfectly. A life of complete uselessness doesn't bother her one little bit. Rise at ten, dress for lunch in the city—at a really good place where the best people are photographed over their lobster—a cocktail party swarming with judges and lawyers, the seating arrangements for a nice little dinner party—my mother fills her life with that sort of thing.'

She stopped abruptly, appalled to hear the bitterness in her voice. There was nothing new about it—she ought to have adjusted to her mother's new life years ago. Perhaps it was the occasional letter, full of praise and pride in her stepchildren, that kept her resentment alive. Kate had somehow never managed to win that kind of approval from her mother, and even now it still hurt. Why on earth had she allowed herself to be drawn into this conversation with Robert Beaumont of all people? He was certainly watching her with great intentness.

'Aren't you being a little hard on her, Kate?'

Of course she was, she knew that. Fiona Malvern could no more help the way she was than the sun could avoid rising every day. She was charmingly superficial, playing at the roles of housewife and mother until she saw the opportunity to play the society hostess to Monte's leading man.

'Probably. Actually I couldn't care less how she spends her time except that her hankerings for that kind of life made my father miserable most of their married life. Then when she left and married Monte—I think it finished him, seeing someone else give her the life that he couldn't.'

Robert watched her fingers twist the stem of the glass first one way, then the other. 'Why did he put up with it?'

'Because he loved her, the poor fool. It was a mismatch from the start, but he was so in love with her

that she used it against him in the end.' Kate stared into
her glass and saw the answer to the question he had
asked her. She was scared stiff of allowing her natural
feelings full rein. There would be no mismatch for her.
No unequal relationship that would leave her vulnerable
and hurt like her father.

'And you have no intention of making your father's
mistake,' Robert said softly.

She looked up, hiding her new self-knowledge. 'No, I
won't.'

'You're not the person to avoid committal to another
for ever, Kate.'

She was really quite proud of her steady hand as she
reached for one of the sandwiches. 'Yes, Andrew said as
much the other night.'

'Young Barrett isn't the man for you,' Robert went
on.

'Oh, I do hope you're wrong. He's invited me to go
away for the weekend with him soon.'

Tension reached out to her, raced around the
luxurious office. 'And will you?'

Kate raised her glass to her mouth and smiled
secretively in answer. They finished their lunch in
silence, then Robert stood up.

'Let me show you around the gallery. You must be
aching to find some monstrosities to justify those
impassioned ideas you aired on television.'

As she rose too, he put a hand to her elbow and she
moved quickly ahead to avoid his touch. 'As to
justification, Mr Beaumont, I'm taking a leaf out of
your book. I refuse to look further than my nose for it.
Down my nose, of course!'

He grinned and she tore her eyes from him. 'Come
now, Kate, isn't that view of me a little out of date?'

It was, but she wasn't willing to accept any other.
That way lay only regret. 'Not at all. Oh, you do have a

certain boyishness at times,' she made it sound quite infantile, 'but you can't disguise the real Robert Beaumont.'

This time she couldn't shake off his hand. Fingers gripping her tightly he guided her into the gallery.

'You haven't seen the real me yet, Kate.'

'Oooh—you mean there's more?'

And he muttered something she didn't catch before he began his tour with her. His gallery held a diverse collection of pieces arranged in harmony for the discriminating buyer. Abstracts and traditional landscapes, portraits and ink drawings complemented each other in their carefully chosen locations. Along with contemporary works were valuable historic paintings and etchings. One or two were very old indeed, dating back to early colonial days when artists had painted their scenes of a new and wild land with the images of a gentler, green England still fresh in their minds. Several watercolours with lengthy histories attached were hung along with a superb Lindsay sketch and the original drawing of an old *Bulletin* cartoon.

'I'm afraid I'm all out of purple crayon nudes right now,' Robert told her gravely, 'I know how disappointed you must be to find none here.'

'I meant that purely as an example, Mr Beaumont. There are some awful pictures sold on signatures alone, as you must know. Evan Gale told me you haven't always endeared yourself to the art élite with your criticisms even of them.'

'Been chatting to Evan, have you? Is he still turning out his commercial masterpieces?'

'Yes, he is. And Galerie Bowman will be staging a showing for him soon.'

Laughter shook his broad shoulders. 'Yes, that would appeal to Evan—to exhibit with a gallery next door to me.'

'That's not his only reason for choosing us, Mr Beaumont,' Kate said sharply, annoyed by his patronising tone. 'It's a business arrangement that will be profitable to both him and us.'

'Of course. What else did Evan say about me?'

'He said he liked you.'

'Which you naturally found hard to believe.'

'And he said you were scrupulously fair . . .'

'How irritating to have my praises sung to you, Kate,' he said dryly.

'I'm beginning to think he might have been right about the last,' she admitted stiffly. 'There does seem to be some evidence of strict impartiality in your pronouncements.'

A small silence followed in which Robert looked down at her as they continued along the gallery.

'Mmm, that's progress of a sort, I suppose. But don't be too swayed by Evan, Kate. I'm not always fair and at times, I'm afraid, not quite impartial.'

Whatever that meant she wasn't sure and had no time to think about it. Robert pointed out a piece of sculpture and quoted a price to raise her eyebrows. 'Another overpriced, exclusive monstrosity for the status-seeking rich,' he added wickedly, baiting her again with her own opinions.

'Exactly what I was thinking,' she told him, but privately she admired the piece, which was magnificent and well worth the money. In fact, she had to admit that everything here was superb. No hint of the mediocre or vulgar for Robert Beaumont's gallery— and nothing so crass as a price tag in sight.

'Do you ever have difficulty finding perfect things for your gallery, Mr Beaumont?' she asked.

'Nothing is ever perfect. I stumble across a gem sometimes only to find it has a flaw. But even flawed perfection can be extremely beautiful.' Kate found his eyes on her and walked hastily ahead, aware of confusion again.

'Do you like this? I've just hung it,' said Robert, and she set startled eyes on her own painting. Re-framed—expensively re-framed—it looked not at all out of place in this rarified setting. Aware of him watching, she managed to suppress all but the initial shock of seeing it there. So now she knew who had so quickly purchased her work on the night of the C.A.G. show.

'You seem to recognise it,' he commented. 'Do you know anything about this artist?'

'No. But—didn't I see it at the C.A.G. exhibition?'

'Yes. It won my Highly Commended.'

'Why did you buy this and not the First or Second Prize pictures?' she fished.

'This has a number of things going for it.' He studied it with her and it was a test to remain detached as he pointed out the features that had won his approval. When he pointed out, just as objectively, a fault, she had a hard time refraining from justification. 'Oh, but what I wanted to achieve there was . . .' she wanted to tell him, but remained silent. As they walked on she glanced back and was filled with elation that Robert unknowingly valued her work enough to hang it in this temple of excellence. How ironic, Kate thought, and her spirits soared. She followed him and it was on the tip of her tongue to tell him right then, but she was still trying to phrase the revelation effectively when he spoke again.

'This is a favourite of mine.' He indicated a peaceful pastoral landscape—a serenely traditional choice, Kate thought, for a critic. 'I might give it to my parents as an anniversary gift.'

'Parents, Mr Beaumont?' she exclaimed in mock surprise, her humour restored by B. Ransome's inclusion on his walls. 'You have a mother and a father?'

He laughed, though she thought there was a trace of irritation in the sound. 'And a brother. They live in Melbourne and I spend some time with them whenever I'm down there.'

Kate mulled over the idea of him with a family like anyone else. He had always seemed such a lone figure. She tried to picture him as a younger man, a boy, suffering pangs of uncertainty and adolescent fears, but couldn't.

'What does your brother do?' she asked, picturing another man like Robert.

'He runs a sports store and has the distinction of being a fine cricketer. He plays for Victoria, which makes Chris Dad's favourite. And having produced two grandchildren for my mother to fuss over, he's several runs ahead of me.'

Kate stared. 'I would have thought *you . . .*'

'Would be number one child?' He shook his head ruefully. 'I'm the elder, but a great disappointment to my father in many ways. He doesn't understand art or why anyone would want a career in it.' He chuckled. 'He would like you, Kate—your challenges to the art establishment echo his sentiments entirely.'

Kate retreated from the idea of being liked and welcomed by Robert's family. Just the words seemed to pull her a little closer to him.

'My mother is more comprehending. I think if I produced a grandchild for her I could redeem myself.' He looked thoughtful for a moment and she wondered if he was thinking of raising a family with Sonia, who didn't look exceptionally maternal. But perhaps the idea of a little boy with dark hair and candid grey eyes would bring out the mother in her. The vision was surprisingly unappealing and she shut it out.

'My mother particularly would like this painting. But Dad might prefer to look at my football trophies.' He grinned at her expression. 'I played for the university—even got the chance to play for Carlton. Dad will never forgive me for letting it go in favour of art. He could have had a hat trick—one son a cricketer, the other a player for his chosen team.'

Kate re-shuffled the jigsaw picture of Robert in her mind. Somehow this other dimension of the man was disturbing. She had images of an appealing little boy with dirty knees and scratches, scruffing about playing football with his brother. Eyes on her, Robert added: 'I was a pest of a kid, always climbing trees and kicking a ball around. I used to fall over a lot and always had scabby knees and bruises.' Kate looked up, startled by the confirmation of her own picture of him. 'But it's a long time since I've fallen flat on my face.'

'Then you're long overdue, Mr Beaumont,' she said lightly, and thought of her picture hanging alongside all these gems.

'That's what I'm afraid of,' he murmured, and they completed their tour. He opened the front doors and showed her the electronic security system that protected his valuable goods. With a rueful air Kate admitted that theirs consisted of an ordinary lock and key and their own presence on the premises.

'That's all you need. You'd hardly be bothered by art thieves with your present stock.'

'You might be surprised,' she said airily, not to be daunted this time by his reference to Galerie Bowman's peasant collection. 'Some middle-class housewives might feel it worthwhile to raid our gallery for something to match their curtains.'

He chuckled and Kate realised how much she liked the sound of it. 'And do you sell to people who want something to fit in with the décor?'

'Actually,' she confided, sure enough of herself now

to admit it, 'someone came in this morning and bought Philip's picture to match her curtains.'

The grey eyes were laughing. 'Too late! What a pity, Kate.'

'Oh, I don't know. This is quite a privilege and one I might not have had otherwise.'

'You could have come here any time Kate, if you were curious.'

'Why should I be curious, Mr Beaumont?'

'You're a woman.' He headed off in the direction of his office again and Kate made a childish face at the arrogant broad back, pulling her muscles quickly into blandness when he turned to usher her through the doorway. 'I have a client calling shortly and have some paperwork to catch up on. Unless someone comes into the gallery you'll be at a loose end.'

'Surely I could handle some office work for you—filing or typing? Did you want to dictate to me?' she asked in wide-eyed innocence. 'I think you'd be awfully good at that.'

Robert sat down at his magnificent desk and idly picked up a pen. Twisting it in his long fingers, he inspected her neat, businesslike figure thoughtfully. In a plain beige skirt and green blouse Kate considered herself to look crisp and efficient. She had pulled her glowing hair back and tied a thin strip of beige silk around it, certain that the effect was demure and unprovocative. But she was careless of the effect of her green eyes, intensified by the colour of the shirt, and unaware that the pulled-back hairstyle merely accentuated the delicate sculpturing of her cheekbones and jaw. With the knowledge of her picture hanging out in Robert's gallery, her eyes sparkled as much with confidence as defiance.

'You seem very philosophical suddenly, Kate.' It was a statement yet invited explanation.

'Do I, Mr Beaumont? Don't worry, I'm sure it won't last all day.'

'I'm sure it won't,' he agreed, and fetched a pad and pencils from the tiny secretary's office opposite his.

The telephone rang once while she was transcribing her notes and she heard his deep, warm voice as he spoke. Once or twice he laughed. She wondered if it was a woman caller—Sonia Marsden perhaps? But it didn't sound like Sonia's name that he used along with his goodbyes. Kate wondered about his love life. Was there more than one woman in it? That he would have his pick was patently obvious. He was cultured, capable, successful—a paradox, surely—an ex-footballer gallery owner and critic. Kate smiled. And she conceded that he had his share—more than his share of physical attraction. Even she had felt the pull of a certain magnetism he possessed, and she was making a conscious effort to resist it.

Yes, women would stand in line for a man like him. Kate pictured a long gallery of women and Robert walking slowly past awarding Commended, Highly Commended, Third, Second and . . . maybe he was hesitating over awarding a First. But his girl-friend Sonia appeared to have no doubt that she would be the major prizewinner.

Kate finished the letters in a sober mood, and clipped them together with copies and envelopes. She heard the arrival of Robert's appointment and their quiet conversation in his office. After a time they left and continued their talk in the gallery.

The phone on the mahogany desk rang again and Kate answered it. It was a man who asked for an appointment with Robert that afternoon.

'Just one moment, I'll check Mr Beaumont's schedule,' she said, and looked around for a diary. Gingerly she tried one of the beautiful hand-made drawers in the desk and found a leather-bound appointments book. A marker opened it at today's date and Kate wrote the man's name down in the empty four o'clock slot. As she finished the call her eyes drifted to the end of the page. Written in black pen was one word—'Kate'.

She stared at it and grew uneasy. It wasn't so odd, she told herself. They had a date for dinner and he had written in her name. But the sight of it there in his handwriting was strangely unsettling.

It was almost three o'clock before he was free again and gave her a sheaf of notes to type. It seemed to be a textbook manuscript and Kate found it direct and brisk. His business might be art, but he wrote about it in a down-to-earth style that would be readily understood by anyone. Where, she wondered, had the pompous style of his letters gone? Especially the first one to them about the sign. That stiff, righteous tone seemed unlike Robert at all now.

While he was busy with another client, a small group of American tourists drew up in the curved drive. A discreet automatic buzz sounded as they entered. Two men and two women, they were viewing the paintings when Kate left the typewriter to speak to them.

They were open and friendly, telling her about their 'wunnerful' holiday in the mountain ranges where they had explored the rain forests.

'We sighted a heap of your amazing birds,' one woman confided. 'Whip-birds and a list of parrots as long as your arm. And those cute little—what were those tiny kangaroo things, Harry—sounds like something you eat . . .?' she demanded of the man next to her, pressing his arm with a well-manicured hand.

'Pademelons, Sophie.'

'That's it. Sweetest little things. Came right out of the forest and let us all but pat them.'

Kate dimpled and smiled as if the local flora and fauna were all her own doing, and after introductions, directed them to a group of paintings by a local man. His subjects included all the elements of the forest—falls, desolate rock faces plunging into tropical growth and close-ups of the magnificent ferns, mosses and orchids that grew in profusion, as Kate informed them, around his hand-built cabin.

'Harry,' said Sophie Brand, 'this one would look great in our bar.' And Harry simply put his hand in his pocket.

Kate promptly removed the picture from the wall. 'One painting sold,' she explained to Robert when he had farewelled his client. 'I need the paperwork. And the other couple are still looking. I think they'll buy, possibly the Lowrey drawing—the old house. Gene and Jo Konowski. Gene's the man, by the way.'

Twenty minutes later the two sales were complete, and the Americans were delighted with the Beaumont Galleries service which included a glass of wine while the second picture was wrapped.

'Robert,' Jo Konowski pronounced it 'Rubbert', 'is Kate your—er—assistant?'

'Just for today,' he told her with his melting smile.

'That's a pity—you make one hell of a team,' her husband said wryly, indicating the two packaged pictures.

'You think so?' Robert looked at Kate with a glimmer of a smile in his eyes.

'Hang on to her—she's a great little salesperson.'

Harry Brand put down his wineglass and Kate reflected that the praise was not quite deserving.

'And sweet with it,' averred Sophie.

'Ah now, I'm well aware of that,' Robert told them. 'Kate's as sweet as wild honey.'

Romantic, Sophie called that. 'Why don't you ever say romantic things like that, Harry darling?'

Harry raised his eyes to the ceiling and they never learned why he omitted to woo Sophie with sweet words. As they left Robert said, 'As you're travelling that way, you might like to see some very good pottery—a small place on your left just a few minutes from here. The paintings are terrible, but the craft is first class.'

'Thank you for the referral,' Kate said stiffly, 'even if it *was* done in your usual arrogant style.'

'You don't imagine that I would recommend your collection to anyone, surely? My neighbourly interest in your gallery doesn't extend to casting aside my principles.'

'Your neighbourly interest doesn't have to be extended at all,' she pointed out, wishing he had never begun his visits to them.

'Your aunt likes me,' he said in smug explanation.

'Well, one out of two is as good as you'll get,' she flared.

'Is that another challenge, Kate?'

'No. A statement of fact.' Already she was regretting her impulsive tongue. His grey eyes were regarding her with a strange mixture of warmth and speculation.

'I daresay I'll survive. It's not the first time I've been rejected by a beautiful woman.'

'The great Robert Beaumont, admitting such a thing! Doesn't your ego tremble at such a revelation?'

Robert regarded her steadily. 'You work so hard at hating, Kate. Would you put as much effort into loving?'

Odd sensations filled Kate. Hate? She didn't hate him.

'You'll never know will you, Mr Beaumont?'

'I might make you eat those words,' he said softly, then added, 'and call me Robert—our station in life isn't that disparate to warrant calling me "Mister".'

'Our station . . .?' Kate put her hands on her hips and glared at him. 'That's not the reason I call you "Mister" . . .' belatedly she saw his amusement and realised she had taken the bait too readily again.

'Why do you?' he asked with interest.

Because just the sound of his given name on her lips conjured up images of the night he had kissed her and showed her that under his arrogance there was fire and steel and a seductive tenderness that had almost made her forget her intention to teach him a lesson. And she *had* forgotten anything else the next time he kissed her.

'Does it matter?' she asked coolly. 'If you really insist, I'll call you Robert.'

'Yes, I do insist.'

CHAPTER SEVEN

At around six, Robert suggested that she dress for their dinner date.

'And you've earned it,' he grinned. 'Two pictures sold is quite an achievement. When you forget your temper you really are a "great little salesperson".'

'Oh, Rubbert,' she drawled, 'should I curtsey or kiss your hand?'

His low laughter followed her to the modern bathroom at the back of the building. She was refreshed by the shower and spent some time applying new make-up and fixing her hair into a loose knot at the back of her head. When she had finished, she saw that it looked rather as she had worn it on that day long ago—only six weeks, actually—when she had driven to the television studio on the mountain expecting to meet a pudgy, balding man with pale hands. Kate met her eyes, smoky green in the artificial light, and was conscious of a vague excitement. Whatever else Robert might or might not be, he was certainly never boring, and the prospect of dinner with him was rather more appealing now than it had been this morning.

The silky copper fabric of the dress and jacket were smoothed into place and she smiled at herself in new calmness. Maybe tonight she would tell him that it was *her* picture hanging in his gallery. And then again, she laughed—she might not. With her skirt and blouse bundled up in her carry-all, she hesitated in the hall, then went to the office.

Robert was at his desk but rose when she stood in the doorway. Despite her striving for nonchalance, she warmed under his scrutiny. The grey eyes roamed her face and moved on to linger on the curves of her long legs, hips and breasts where the clinging material was at its most loving. Perversely now she wished she hadn't worn it.

He came over to her and took the larger bag, and Kate was certain that she was overdressed when she saw that he was still wearing his casual day clothes.

'Shall we go?' He took her arm and guided her outside where he performed the final precautions to activate the security system.

In the low white car, Kate sank into the comfortable upholstery and opened her bag to withdraw her clutch purse. By the time she looked up they had turned into the long drive to Robert's house. He turned his head at the moment she became aware and said: 'I said dinner afterwards. I didn't, if you recall, say where.'

Stiltedly she said: 'We're having dinner at your house?'

He merely nodded, but a smile lingered on his mouth as the car slowed between established native gardens, and slid under cover. The house was barely distinguishable from the environment. The many-faceted walls could easily be sharp-edged rocks among the trees, ferns and shrubs. Concealed spotlights lit the walkway from the garage into the house, and Kate barely noticed the entrance, so engrossed was she with her thoughts.

Alarm bells were ringing in her head and she saw again those bold black letters—'Kate'—in his diary. But what could she do now that would not look like some undignified—not to mention frightened—retreat? With chin up she followed him until he stood aside to usher her through the door, and passed him hoping that he wouldn't see her apprehension. She was thinking how very easily he had woven his spell about her in a grotty little garden shed and how much more vulnerable she

was on his home ground. Even so she shelved her
worries on that score moments later as they entered a
large room and Robert switched on the lights. Kate's
gasp of pleasure was involuntary.

'Oh yes,' she said, before she could stop herself.

He paused, his hand still on the switch. 'You
approve, Kate?'

She noticed the amusement in his tone, but her
attention was occupied with the beautiful room. Its
vast carpeted expanse was broken into several levels
and areas, yet without destroying the feeling of space. A
chrome and glass dining setting was placed in the angle
of the wall and the clean modern lines of two settees
faced each other behind a partial wall and screen of
plants. The rest of the space was sparsely furnished with
big, comfortable chairs, low tables and built-in
bookshelves on one huge inset between the glass panels
of the end wall. The entire side wall of the room was
natural rock, lit from above by a line of recessed lights.
Kate's gaze returned to Robert.

'Yes, this is right.' She hurried on, 'I mean—it looks
like you. But your office at the gallery doesn't.'

He was watching her, arms folded and shoulder
against the wall so that his body was at an angle. 'Very
perceptive. The office is furnished for the clients. What
is there about this,' he lifted a hand and waved it
casually about the room, 'that looks like me?'

Kate regarded the glass floor-to-ceiling windows
curtained by nothing more than the lush gardens
outside, secretive in the exterior lights that penetrated
only the upper leaves and branches. She looked at the
superb, austere lines of the furniture. 'Taste,' she told
him, 'and no frills.' Her eyes went to the rock wall.
'And that,' she pointed, '*that* reminds me strongly of
you.'

'Unkind, Kate. In the right hands I'm merely putty.'

He pushed himself upright again and turned another switch. The angled wall to Kate's left was illuminated and she could see a large painting on it. Curiously she walked out into the room to view it, conscious of her host's eyes on her. The picture was unusual. Striking in its form and colour, it took some moments to see that it was in fact a modern interpretation of the age-old theme of mother and child.

'A woman painted this, I'll be——' she caught the last word back and flicked a glance at him. She'd almost said 'bet' again.

'You're learning,' he said provokingly. 'But this time you're right. The artist was a woman.'

She moved closer and he came and stood beside her, looking at the canvas. The artist's signature was sprawled in one corner—just a first name, 'Dyan.'

'Did you know her?' asked Kate, guessing that he had by the reflective gleam in his eyes. He shifted them suddenly from the picture to her.

'Woman's intuition, Kate? Yes, I knew her. She painted this just for me.' His voice was dry and Kate wondered curiously if the painter had been important to him, or still was.

'As a reminder?'

He gave a laugh of sorts. 'You could say that. A reminder and a farewell.' Abruptly he went and picked up her bag. Come on, Kate, I'll show you where you can leave your things and comb your already perfect hair.'

As they moved away, she took another look at the Madonna. Maybe he hadn't been joking about a rejection.

They entered another wing of the house and Robert pushed open a door to a small guest room. 'Leave your things here. The bathroom is through the swing doors. I'm going to shower and change now. If you like to go back to the living room you'll find a drink waiting for you. Feel free to explore my home, Kate.'

Curiously she did walk around, sipping the drink she had found on the bar. She made her way to the foyer, remembering Sonia Marsden's penchant for the tall amphora. She was wrong, Kate decided as she viewed the restrained placement of a piece of sculpture and a Chinese pot of papyrus. There was nothing more needed in the small area, and the bulk of the pot Sonia had admired would most certainly be out of place. Robert might have to be very tactful with the girl if they married and found their tastes in conflict. Her mood dived downwards as she went to look again at the picture by 'Dyan'. Who was she, she wondered, and to what part of Robert's life had she belonged? But the picture, painted with sure, energetic strokes told her only that the woman who had painted it had been strong, determined. Kate tore herself away from the fruitless speculation and looked at Robert's collection of treasures. Niches in a half wall that bound the conversation area, were the perfect display cases for several beautiful objects. A carved statuette that looked Greek and ancient stood in one, looking just as perfect in the austere setting as it might have in its original home. A set of carved quartz chessmen filled another niche, and with a glow of pleasure she saw that Louise's naiad ewer was displayed in solitary splendour. They weren't doing too badly, Kate thought, and smiled. Louise's work in Robert's home and her own in his gallery. Robert didn't know it, but they were advancing on him.

She ran a finger along the smooth shelf edge and admired the grouping of several other small objects, all in immaculate order and flawless. Robert's passion for excellence didn't stop with his work. Not so much a job, she thought, laughing softly, but a way of life.

The glass dining table was set for two—close together at one end she noticed and she had smelt something cooking when she'd glanced in at the super kitchen. His housekeeper must have prepared everything—she viewed the awesome job of cleaning the place—he obviously must have a housekeeper. Perhaps, Kate's spirits rose, she was somewhere in the house and they weren't alone after all. But as she became aware of soft music piping into the room, she knew there was no one else here. Just her—and Robert. She put down the drink, feeling suddenly nervous.

This was a heady atmosphere in which to find herself with a man like Robert. Kate's boy-friends had been easy-going students with as little money to spare as they had panache. She was out of her depth here with a man who was used to the best—and to having things his own way.

But Robert came back from his shower relaxed and pleasant and apparently determined to make her feel the same way. He had changed into dark trousers and a white silk shirt patterned in a small red and black design.

'Another drink, Kate?' he smiled, and took the glass from her fingers to mix drinks at the bar. Over them he made such easy, innocuous conversation that Kate's nerves quietened, helped just a bit, she thought, by the two drinks. Even so, she had a yearning for a small table at a restaurant—and people. Lots of people.

'Would you care to be seated, Kate?' he asked when she had refused a third drink, and escorted her to the table. 'I'm host and waiter tonight,' and as she sat in the chair he pulled out for her, laid a napkin across her knees with a flourish. 'Yours to command, in fact.' He disappeared into the kitchen and emerged with an ice bucket and a bottle of wine. Another trip produced an avocado and crab entrée.

'Delicious,' said Kate, sampling it. 'Your housekeeper is very versatile. I imagine it was she who made the food for tonight?'

'Most of it. But this I made myself. I'm regarded as a pretty fair cook, actually,' he grinned.

'Is there no end to your talents, Robert?' she mocked.

'There must be, I suppose, Kate,' he told her modestly, 'but I keep surprising myself.'

He brought in the second course, carrying a heavy earthenware pot in his oven-mittened hands. Kate watched him lower the dish to the heat-resistant mat, bemused by the sight of those large hands shrouded in quilted, beflowered fabric. It was too much for her. She burst out laughing and he looked at her for an explanation.

'It's those,' she pointed to the mittens still encasing his hands, 'they make you look——' she laughed again.

'Ridiculous?' he suggested. 'Henpecked?' He stripped off the oven gloves.

'Not henpecked—never that. Or ridiculous. Just—oh, human, I suppose.'

'I'm very human, Kate—you should know that.' The words effectively shrank the remaining smile about her mouth. She gazed apprehensively at the wine glasses, the cosy setting for two, heard the mellow music of guitars coming from the ceiling speakers and hoped that he wouldn't prove it to her tonight as he had done before.

As he ladled the food on to her plate, talking in a casual impersonal way, Kate relaxed. He didn't sound like a man with seduction on his mind. But then with Robert Beaumont she was never sure. With Robert, she was always guessing.

'This is wonderful!' she exclaimed, sampling the chicken cooked in the French provincial way with mushrooms and wine. They drank an excellent chilled

white wine with it—dry and with a superior edge to it.
A true Beaumont choice. But she resisted the urge to
tell him so, confining herself to polite observations and
answers to his occasional questions. Unobtrusively he
refilled her glass so that the level of her wine hardly
dropped, and it wasn't until she found herself smiling
with unusual warmth at him that Kate realised she was
drinking more than usual. Firmly she ignored the wine
from then on, annoyed with herself for allowing even
the slightest dulling of her senses.

'Why did you tell me to dress up,' she asked, 'if you
knew you'd be bringing me here?'

'I didn't tell you to dress up.'

'But you said to wear something formal.'

'No, I said to wear that.' He ran his eyes over the
silky dress that emphasised her figure. 'And nothing
surprises me more than that you did.'

'Why this one?'

'Fishing for compliments, Kate? Because I liked
you in it at Clarry's party.' He looked directly into
her eyes. 'You were more beautiful that night than
when I first saw you—and I didn't think that was
possible.'

Forgetting her resolution, Kate picked up her wine
glass and drank, remembering that party. Harsh words
had been exchanged between them that night and he
had held her for the first time. She almost choked on
the wine as the thought entered her mind. Why on earth
should she find that brief dance with him a sort of
milestone? He had offered himself as the experienced
lover he thought she needed then, and had been almost
brutally frank about her initial attraction to him. How
could she have forgotten that? Kate gulped more wine
as something akin to panic set in. She had successfully
kept him at arms length for so long, yet here she was,
alone with him on his own luxurious ground. She

should have made some excuse and run when she'd seen her name in his diary. Now it seemed less of a reminder than a promise or a threat. 'I intend to win the battle,' he had said grimly to her on yet another night when he had held her again in greater intimacy.

The silence stretched out between them, Kate feverishly planning how she might get away from this close atmosphere while Robert helped himself to more chicken.

'Kate?' he held the lid of the dish, the server ready.

She shook her head. 'No more, thank you. It was delicious.' Maybe, she thought, she could throw up. That would put a damper on any scene of seduction. Or she could faint. No—no. Her cheeks burned at the scene that conjured up. Robert bending to lift her body into his arms and laying her down somewhere . . . no. Definitely not a faint. Could she walk home? Find her way down the hill in the dark—but he would follow her and—with a sudden chill she remembered that Louise wouldn't be home tonight. Suspiciously she glanced at the dark head opposite.

No. Get a grip on yourself, Kate. He couldn't have arranged Louise and Max's love life to suit himself. But it was an amazing coincidence that Robert always seemed to have more than his share of advantages.

'Tell me, Kate, have you ever heard anything about a painter called Ransome?'

With her head full of suppressed panic and in retreat from him, Kate stared uncomprehendingly. She almost said, 'That's me.'

'The artist whose picture you bought from the C.A.G.?' she stalled, trying not to reveal just how well acquainted she was with B. Ransome. It would be intriguing to know what he would say about it first.

He nodded and finished his meal, to give her his full attention. 'Yes, that's the one. He needs some guidance, but his work is a little out of the ordinary. I'd like to see more of it. What was your assessment of it?'

'Oh—er——' Kate was aware of the incongruity of the situation. That he asked her opinion at all was surprising, but that it concerned her own work gave her the oddest feeling of superiority. 'I liked it. But I didn't think it good enough to earn your approval.'

'Then we both liked it. We're making progress if we've found something on which we agree.'

She almost giggled. 'Yes, Robert. I'd have to say that Ransome is my kind of painter.'

He raised his wineglass to his mouth and drank. 'I have a feeling the one in the gallery will be sold soon. Someone is very interested. If you hear anything about Ransome let me know, will you?'

He was very certain that Ransome was a man, Kate thought. 'If I heard where he was I might want his work for *my* gallery,' she told him, trying to keep a straight face.

'I doubt your customers could afford his prices, Kate, so you might as well stick to your own kind of—er—suppliers.'

She blinked. What a fraud he was! He had picked her painting up for a song and here he was trying to pretend it was out of her reach so that she wouldn't intrude on his territory. She was delighted to catch him out—what a pity she couldn't tell him what a liar he was. Confidence seeped back into her. A buyer for her work at Beaumont Galleries! And Robert eager to get more of them. She was tempted to tell him airily that she might—just *might* be able to contact the artist for him after all, but restrained herself. She was enjoying too much the private feeling of advantage it gave her. And, she reflected, it wasn't often she ever had any where Robert was concerned.

'I can't promise to turn a new talent over to you,

Robert. In fact, I might just enjoy "discovering" him first.'

'*I* discovered him first,' Robert reminded her gently, not taking her threat seriously, 'and I can't imagine you have time to indulge in a scramble to locate him. Leave the "real art" to me, Kate, and canvass a few housewives for their calendar copies for your place.' He grinned at her glittering expression, then looked mildly suspicious when she acquiesced with a meek,

'Yes, Robert.'

He cleared away the second course and brought a creamy gateau to the table. Kate stared. 'I would have thought you were a cheese and crackers man. Are you actually going to eat that?'

Flicking her a glance as he sliced it, he murmured, 'Yes. I fancy a taste of honey now and then.'

'Too much sweetness isn't good for you, Robert,' she said pertly, unperturbed for once by his undertones.

He laughed and put a plate in front of her. 'I have hardly any lately. Not nearly enough to satisfy my sweet tooth.'

'Too bad.' There was always Sonia, she thought, to bring a little sweetness into his life, but she decided against mentioning that.

'Yes,' he looked mournful, 'isn't it?'

After dessert they moved to the lounge for coffee and liqueurs.

'Why did you open a gallery here, Robert?' she asked, thinking he would be more at home in the cosmopolitan surroundings of Melbourne or Sydney.

'The place itself. Three years ago I fell in love with the mountains. I bought the gallery and then built the house. Unfortunately I have to divide my time between my gallery here and the one I have in Melbourne. But this is home for me now.'

He described his business in Melbourne briefly,

giving her the impression of a small gallery on a busy street in the city proper. Without him saying, Kate knew it would be in its way as beautiful as the gallery down the long drive.

'Does Dyan live in Melbourne?' she asked innocently.

'What——?' His eyes narrowed on her. 'Curious about my past, Kate? Or just my past women?'

'Your past women—plural—are of no interest to me,' she said distastefully, 'but I am interested in one with the discrimination to turn you down—if that's what she did.'

His knuckles paled and his fingers tightened about the glass he was holding. 'Yes, she turned me down a long time ago.'

A fleeting pain crossed his face and Kate regretted her sarcasm. The idea of Robert being vulnerable enough to be hurt created an odd sensation in her chest.

'I'm sorry—I shouldn't have mentioned it.'

'You shouldn't say a lot of things, Kate.' His voice was harsh, edgy. 'You'll say something you'll regret for ever one day.'

He sounded as if he knew from personal experience, and Kate's heart plunged unaccountably. Who was it who had taught him that—Dyan, or one of his other 'past women' or Sonia? Chastened, she went to look again, absently this time, at his collection of expensive ornaments. After a while he came to tell her about each one, his tanned face showing no trace of his former anger.

'Are you rich, Robert?' she enquired as she pondered on the cost of all these things. His house, car and clothes looked like those of a wealthy man, but maybe he was like a lot of others and simply lived beyond his means. After all, it was an expensive business he was in. There was a peculiar look on his face at her question.

'I suppose you could say that. Am I more interesting, more attractive as a rich man?'

Kate laughed. 'Interesting? You'd be interesting if you were a swagman!'

'Thank you.' He sketched a slight bow.

'Don't mention it. Cobras are interesting too.' But if she hoped to dash him, she was disappointed. He laughed out loud.

'As for attractive—I don't find you any more attractive now that I know you've pots of money.' It wasn't saying much, she thought. She'd already found him overpoweringly attractive. Wealth could add no superlatives to that.

'Ah, well, one out of two isn't bad,' he grinned, and Kate remembered that she'd said something like that earlier. But their unfriendly exchanges seemed suddenly harder to recall. At this rate she could well end up liking him. The idea filled her with uneasiness. Physical attraction hit like a hammer and she knew when she was being attacked by that. But liking—that could creep up unawares, and before she knew it, liking could turn to . . .

'Do you paint, Kate?' asked Robert, and she looked at him, startled.

'I—dabble,' she said carefully, and smiled, thinking she could tell him just what kind of dabbling she did.

'And?' he prompted.

'Oh, you know—lots of people try painting, but hardly any are any good.' She was strangely reluctant to tell him an outright lie. Even her evasive generalisation made her feel guilty.

'I'm amazed to hear you say that, since you're hellbent on displaying the work of talentless dabblers in your gallery.'

'They're not talentless,' she defended. 'Just untrained or under-trained.'

'Talent or not, what I dislike is that their early work, which is atrocious, should be sold off to unsuspecting customers. At their stage of progress, they should be prepared to accept years of work before they produce anything saleable.'

Kate warmed to her topic. 'But don't you see? The people who buy them are at the same stage.' She had his complete attention and rose to walk about between the two settees making her points with telling gestures of her hands. 'Of all the millions of people interested in art only a handful have expert knowledge. Some are expert exponents and some are expert evaluators. What about all the rest?'

She whirled about and silky fabric of her skirt flipped to reveal a flash of one curved thigh. Unaware, she sat down again on the edge of the settee opposite him. Her body leaned forward and her hands spread expressively.

'I think that for every stratum of proficiency in art there's a matching stratum among those who can't *do* but admire. And maybe, without expert training, they have to experience each stratum before being able to appreciate the next. Like—a—a baby,' she added in sudden inspiration. Robert's eyebrows flew up in surprise and a smile hovered at the corners of his mouth. 'At first a baby only likes milk. And if it's never offered anything else in infancy it will dislike other foods and have difficulty adjusting to their taste. But the mother offers it rice cereal and it learns to eat that, then vegetables and so on until eventually it can appreciate a wide variety of foods. But if it grows up to become a gourmet, it will have no cravings for rice cereal, because it was simply a step along the way to a mature appreciation.'

Kate sat back in the luxurious comfort of the settee and reached absently for her liqueur. She was warm from riding her pet hobbyhorse and her throat was dry. She took a mouthful of the drink, and another, then realised her mistake when a slow fire began to burn in her stomach.

Robert watched her with a curious expression. She choked down the flames in her throat and looked back, wondering what he was thinking. In the discreetly low lights she couldn't be sure. She glanced around—surely the lighting had been stronger than this earlier?

'What you're saying, then, is that those pictures you have down there all have potential buyers at a similar stage of development as the painters?'

She nodded, almost suffocating from the heat in her throat.

'That would make Philip's work the equivalent of—er—rice cereal, according to your allegory.'

'Do you think I could have a drink?' she croaked, resigned at the knowing grin on his mouth.

'You shouldn't toss down a liqueur like that. You'll get drunk.'

He rose and went to the bar to pour a drink. With his back to her she couldn't see what it was, but when he handed her a long glass clinking with ice cubes and Coke she took it gratefully. After a soothing draught, she returned to his last comment.

'Yes, Philip's picture is one of the more basic ones. But it did find a buyer. Admittedly she bought it to match her curtains . . .'

'Purple?' he winced, recalling the unusual colour of the landscape.

'Yes.' She ignored his expression of distaste. 'But eventually she'll be dissatisfied with it and the next picture she buys will be subtly better. Who knows, one day the metamorphosis may be complete and Mrs Price might walk into Beaumont Galleries for some "genuine art".'

'In effect, you claim to be educating future clients for me?' His shoulders shook a little as he considered this piece of naïveté.

'You may laugh, but you're wrong if you think

people will be educated to appreciate art without experiencing different levels of it.'

'You didn't say all this on television,' he pointed out.

'It's a miracle I said anything. Unlike you, I hadn't been on TV before and it was unnerving.' *You* were unnerving, she thought, remembering the occasion.

He got up and took her empty glass. 'Another?'

She nodded thirstily.

'You looked cool and beautiful. No need to feel you failed—you did manage to get in a few punches you know.'

Yes, Kate thought, and ignored the careless compliment. But not the knock-out punch that Robert had landed. She stayed silent taking the drink from him and sliding her fingers quickly from contact with his. The Coke was deliciously cold as she took several gulps from the tall glass.

'Come,' he held out a hand to her and she took it and stood without thinking, 'I want to show you something.' His smile deepened at her immediate resistance. 'I keep some paintings up here at the house when the Gallery storeroom is crowded. I thought you might like to see them.'

She looked around. Where would they be? she thought uneasily.

'They're hung in the games room,' he told her, and waited for her reaction. Kate didn't like the sound of that at all—she kept thinking of her name in the diary. 'And I didn't say "etchings",' he reminded her with a wicked smile. 'I'll freshen our drinks and take them with us.' He smoothly removed her glass and took it to the bar. Kate was almost perspiring, she was so warm— and she took off her jacket. As he handed her the refilled glass his grey eyes ran quickly over her bare shoulders, but he moved away without comment and she followed.

The games room was a large, square area under a raked ceiling supported by heavy beams. An enormous billiards table stood at one end under a long, fringed light fitting. At the other end was built a nineteenth-century style pub bar complete with a huge painting of a reclining nude above it. The fittings were all brass and the front of the bar was decorated and curlicued as if it was the genuine thing. Which, of course, she should have guessed, it was. Reclaimed Robert told her, from a San Franciscan hotel being demolished. Although, he said, the original had been much longer. This was a composite of the best preserved bits re-assembled for this room.

'You should have freshened our drinks in here,' she said looking at the well stocked bar.

'Ah, but you might have been thirsty along the way,' was his grave reply, a teasing reminder of her foolhardiness in throwing down the liqueur to create the heat and thirst that consumed her.

In this room, too, there was comfortable seating, but this time red plush settees in the same period as the bar. In surprise she noticed three pin-ball machines along the wall, under a couple of the paintings that he had brought her to see. Old-fashioned machines, their decoration an art form in itself, they looked incredibly right for the room yet all wrong for Robert. Frivolous and carnival-like in their garish colours, they seemed too much fun for his elegant background. But then her early images of Robert were shattering in almost every direction.

A piano was set up on an angle near the bar—an old instrument that looked to be turn-of-the-century bar-room vintage.

'All that's missing is some honky-tonk or ragtime,' Kate commented as they walked across the thick cream carpet.

'You want music, Kate sweetheart,' Robert inclined his head in a mock bow, 'you shall have it. Come and lean on the piano in the time-honoured tradition and I'll play for you.'

'You play the piano?' she echoed, warmed by the mock endearment and the teasing look in his eyes.

'Why, of course.' He led her to the old upright and she put her drink on top of it and watched him through the fronds of a fern that perched there in a brass pot.

Robert flexed his fingers and assumed a serious expression as he laid his hands to the keyboard. A Scott Joplin melody filled the room, and Kate raised her eyebrows as the uncomplicated opening bars progressed to a complex piece of jazz performed unerringly. His eyes met hers briefly, questioningly as if he was asking, 'Well, how is it?' Perfect, she thought then saw the quiver of his broad shoulders. Perhaps *too* perfect. She walked around to stand behind him and he looked up at her. His hands failed to keep up with the keyboard which played on unaided.

'You fraud, Robert Beaumont!' she exclaimed, laughter bubbling up. Unconsciously she put a hand on his shoulder, watching the notes play in ghostly perfection.

'I thought you'd rout me sooner, Kate.' His grey eyes were boyish with mischief. He looked young and endearing, and Kate's defences lowered.

'I should have,' she admitted. 'After studying the piano for ten years as a child.'

'You play? Sit down and play something for me.'

'But it's a pianola.'

'It's dual. You can play it as a piano too.' He made room on the polished seat and Kate sat with a show of reluctance.

'After all this time I'm probably rusty,' she warned, then: 'Do you prefer Chopin or Liszt?'

'Chopin.'

Nervously she curled and uncurled her fingers, threw him a fugitive glance and poised her hands above the keys. Then she lowered her two index fingers and gave a faultless performance of 'Chopsticks'.

His laughter ran out long before she had finished and his arm dropped to her shoulders on the final flourish.

'Hoist with my own petard! No piano lessons?' he asked.

'No piano lessons. But I learned to play a mean recorder and spent my spare time running.'

'Running?' They rose and walked across to a group of pictures, Robert's arm still about her.

'Four hundred metres junior school champion two years in a row,' she grinned. 'But by the time I reached senior school I'd slowed down and only managed a few second and third placings.'

'And now?'

'Now I've slowed right down. I don't run at all.'

'Don't you?' he said softly, and laughed. 'That's a pity. You could run with me.'

'You'd be too fast for me, Robert.' She had a fuzzy feeling that they had stopped talking about running, but couldn't trace the point of departure.

'Quite the contrary. I'm having a hard time catching up.'

CHAPTER EIGHT

KATE heard the echo of the words Robert had said to her that first time they met—'I'm in the mood for a chase,' but they failed to alarm her now as a growing weakness held her at his side, returning his smile as he guided her around the perimeter of the big room. She looked at the art and heard him talking, but none of the words meant anything, only the rich, deep cadences of his voice which coloured her consciousness of him. Music was throbbing around them now, suddenly up-tempo. Fancy, she thought dreamily, Robert could have George Benson's guitar strumming through the speakers in every room in this fantastic house—the kitchen, living room—bedroom ... 'What?' Kate stared up at Robert as he spoke. He's the best-looking man I've ever met, she thought, amazed that she had never told herself that before.

'Would you like to play the machines?' he repeated, his eyes warm and friendly. She smiled and nodded. She was feeling warm and friendly herself and inordinately confused about it. Blinking, she focused on the painted pin-ball monster. Robert showed her how to operate it, pulling out the lever and snapping it back to send the metal balls shooting around the board. His score rolled up on to the machine accompanied by the ringing of bells. 'You try,' he said, and moved slightly aside to let her use the lever. His other arm went to brace himself on the gilt-painted edge of the machine as he helped her twist the reluctant lever from its socket and Kate was neatly trapped, his arms making a barrier on either side. She felt warmer than ever and kept very still, concentrating on the game to distract herself from his closeness behind her. Her score rang up, but so great was her agitation that she couldn't separate the ringing in her head from the pealing of the machine.

'Very good,' he said near her ear, and his breath warmly disturbed the hair at her temple. Assuming they would move on, Kate turned and discovered too late that he had scarcely shifted, just enough to receive her into his arms, which closed about her with alacrity. Her eyes flew to his face, startled and dismayed by her instant reactions to the feel of him against her.

'You want to dance, Kate?' he asked, mockingly tender, and pulled her closer to move around the room to the music that was pouring down from the speakers.

She didn't even try to stop it. Her first feeble effort to stay aloof was abandoned as she gave herself up to the weakening sensation of being in his arms. She closed her eyes. Robert's arms were strong and safe around her and she rested her dizzy head against his smooth cheek, grateful for his support. Around and around he took her until she was no longer conscious of moving her legs, relying on him completely to hold her and guide her.

When his lips came down on hers it seemed a logical extension of their slow revolutions about the room. As the music flowed in brilliant, silver phrases, they whirled until Kate lost all orientation. Where she was no longer mattered—what had happened in the past was unimportant. There was only now. Nothing but the strength of the arms surrounding her, nothing but the scent of him, the tender dominance of his mouth as he teased her lips apart. In wonder she slid her hands over the planes of his back, explored the shape of him through the silk texture of his shirt.

One of his hands loosened the pins in her hair and as if from a vast distance, Kate felt the brush of it on her bare shoulders. Still they danced, Robert's mouth moving from hers to bring alive the susceptible curve of her neck, the hollow of her throat. She put up a hand to his thick, springy hair and ran her fingers through it. 'Mmm,' she murmured, 'I always wanted to do that.' Dimly she heard the voice—the woman's voice. It sounded throaty and sensuous and she only recognised it as her own when she spoke again.

Robert had pulled away from her a little, looking down at her, and she slid her arms about his neck.

'Don't let me go,' she said, and heard the words seconds after they left her mouth.

'I won't,' he told her huskily.

Her mind was in a spiral as Robert bent and picked her up and the raked, raftered ceiling circled by. He lowered her to one of the red plush settees and his head blotted out the rafters. She reached up and drew him down to her, smiling at his handsome face and passionate grey eyes. One finger traced the bridge of his straight nose and moved across his cheek.

'I shouldn't have hit you,' she whispered, and put her lips to his face where the awful red mark of her hand had branded him. Her movement seemed to set him afire. His kisses grew long and demanding, his hands more searching, more intimate. Kate was overwhelmed by him. This wonderful new feeling she had for him overcame all her restraint and her head spun under the assault on her senses. When his hands gently turned down the top of her strapless dress to touch her breasts, she arched her back in invitation. It was all new—no one had touched her like this. She had never wanted anyone to do so. And now, as his hands and mouth moved over the pale skin of her breasts, she knew that she would never want anyone else but him to touch her in this way. Her head was suddenly clear, her eyes wide in absolute honesty. How could she have so long denied the truth?

Her hands were in his hair. 'Robert ...' she whispered, wanting to say something but not really knowing what. Closing her eyes, she felt his mouth on her throat. 'I don't want tonight to end,' she said inadequately.

He raised his head and his body was stock still. 'It doesn't have to,' he said in a low voice, and Kate tried to interpret his strange expression as he stared at her flushed, vulnerable face. 'Stay the night, Kate?' he murmured, lowering his head so that his mouth brushed hers as he spoke. 'Stay with me until morning.'

In complete surrender Kate wrapped her arms about his neck. She had known this all the time. How stubborn she had been to pretend it could be otherwise!

'Yes—yes, until morning.' And now she heard her own voice clearly, aware that she was committing herself utterly to him.

'Kate ...'

She heard him draw a deep breath, then his warmth left her and she lay on the settee holding up a hand to him. She was smiling still, her green eyes languid and dreamy from his lovemaking and the low lights shone gently on the curves of her shoulders and breasts. She made no effort to cover herself—just held up her hand to bring him back. But slowly as he looked down at her, his breathing fast and his eyes unreadable, her imploring hand withdrew and the green eyes shed their daze in gradual dawning. Her soft mouth was still parted from his kisses and began to tremble. The light gleamed on the sudden moisture welling in her eyes and she closed them momentarily against the roving of his over her disarray. At last she understood.

With shaking hands she adjusted her dress and sat up, feeling soiled and sick.

'Kate ...' Robert said again, and made a move to touch her but she flinched aside.

It had been a salutary lesson from a master, one she

wouldn't forget. He had made her own daring deceit in his arms that night after the exhibition seem like mere childishness. He remained standing beside the settee, saying nothing but watching her trembling hand push back her hair, smooth her dress over her hips. When she rose with as much dignity as she could muster, she looked directly into his eyes.

'You said you'd win the battle,' she said in a strangled voice, and shook off his hands as he reached for her.

'Kate, that wasn't why . . .' he began, and she laughed, the sound brittle in the silence.

'Heavens, you warned me often enough, didn't you, Robert? What was the last warning? "You'll say something you'll regret for ever"? But don't imagine that *you* warrant for ever!'

She turned away quickly just in time as her voice broke on the last word. But the tears hadn't come when she found the room to collect her bags. She hurried out, avoiding the mirror completely. She didn't want to see the shreds of the person called Kate Bowman.

For of course Robert had won. Somehow she had forgotten her own instinct for caution—somehow she had fallen in love and had it thrown back at her all in one night. She was the loser, though Robert might never, *must* never know by just how much. In the living room she picked up her jacket and put it on.

He was waiting, big and powerful and wearing a closed look.

'Would you please take me home?' Kate said through stiff lips, but politely—oh, so politely, addressing the stranger he had always been.

He nodded, hands pushed into his pockets and head back, looking at her through half-closed eyes.

'We'll discuss this tomorrow, Kate.'

A small, set smile moved her mouth. 'No, Mr Beaumont, we won't.'

He drove her the short distance down the mountain road in silence. As she took her bags from him at the door she said coldly, 'I thought you might like to know that I hated myself for behaving the way I did when you called here that night. As soon as I could bring myself to mention my disgusting behaviour I intended to apologise. But it's hardly necessary now, is it? I think you would have to agree that you've out-performed me.'

He didn't answer and was there, standing at the door, when she closed it in his immobile face.

Louise arrived home around nine the following morning in the benign golden sunshine. Her initial awkwardness disappeared as Kate tactfully avoided her eyes for a few minutes, concentrating on polishing the gallery floor.

'Enjoy yourself, Louise?' she called over her shoulder, and reflected that, in the circumstances, the conventional question was perhaps not the right one.

'Very nice,' was Louise's cautious reply. But as Kate got to her feet and turned to her aunt, she saw the real answer on her face. Louise wore a delicate flush on her cheeks and her eyes were soft and dreamy. Yes, thought Kate with a flash of warmth in her frozen heart, Louise had enjoyed herself.

'And what about you?' The older woman went to put her bag away in the bedroom and called the question as she went.

'Not bad, considering I was in the company of His Lordship,' Kate answered flippantly, glad that Louise could not see her face. Not that she looked angry or felt angry. Just dead. Last night seemed to have killed all the emotion in her—even her resentment, anger, hate— everything she had thought she'd felt for Robert. Even that new, mind-shattering feeling she had only discovered last night was gone—but she knew somehow that that was only temporary. Last night she had lain in her bed staring into the darkness and feeling nothing. Just a heavy weight inside her taking the place of all feeling.

It had been a relief when daylight came and she could set herself tasks to occupy her body. The cleaning and polishing motions reminded her that she was alive after all. Now the strenuous activity, coupled with her unaccustomed drinking of the night before, had taken its toll and she was burnt out, exhausted by her lack of sleep. But Kate was determined that Louise should not guess at her state and followed her to talk as naturally as she could.

'Did four Americans call in here yesterday?'

'Yes, they did—and bought a heap of pottery. They said Robert sent them.' She smiled. 'It's very good of him to refer customers to us.'

Kate casually turned to flip through the clothes hanging in her wardrobe, keeping her face averted. 'Not so marvellous in the circumstances. I'd just sold a painting for him and gave him a tip for a second sale, so he was feeling grateful. But he might do it on a regular basis, Louise, if you asked him. For the pottery, I mean. He wouldn't refer his worst enemy here for a picture.'

'You still don't—like him, Kate?'

She flung a smile at her aunt. 'Like? No, he's not a man that I like, Louise.' How true, she thought grimly. Liking had, after all, crept up on her and overtaken her. 'But I think I understand him better now.' True again.

'He must have been impressed when you made some sales for him?'

'He did say thank you.'

'Where did you go for dinner?' asked Louise.

Kate averted her face again. 'A bit of a surprise, really. We went to his house.'

Louise's silence was eloquent. 'Oh yes?' she said eventually. 'I imagine it's quite beautiful.'

'It is. He had your naiad jug in his living room, Lou—in the very good company of his other treasures.'

'Yes, he said he was something of a collector.'

He'd gained an unexpected addition to his collection last night, Kate reflected. Thank heavens he didn't know it.

Louise emptied her overnight bag and glanced sheepishly at Kate when she picked up a garment that unfolded in her hand to reveal the soft fabric and lace of a nightgown.

'Nice,' Kate commented. 'I'll bet Max liked that!'

Her aunt folded it quickly. A sweet smile curved her mouth. 'He did,' she said simply.

'Louise, that painting of mine that was sold . . . it was Robert who bought it for his gallery.'

'Kate, that's wonderful! He must value it very highly to hang it in his place. Congratulations, my dear.' She surveyed Kate's introspective expression. 'You didn't tell him it was yours, did you?'

'No. I intended to last night but—didn't get around to it. I don't think it matters much. I suppose I'll tell him one of these days. You can tell him if you like.'

Louise held up both hands. 'Oh no, B. Ransome! You can do your own dirty work. He might not be too pleased that it's taken you so long to let him know— and I don't intend to be on the receiving end of Robert's displeasure.'

'Coward,' said Kate, smiling faintly and wondering how she had ever considered that her Ransome identity gave her an advantage over Robert. She knew from her father's experience that loving someone gave *them* all the advantages. Only last night she had been revelling in her private one-upmanship. Now the secret seemed pathetic in the light of the evening's conclusion.

She decided to take the car and deliver Philip's cheque for his painting in person. In view of the blow delivered to his self-esteem by that first ill-fated purchase for which Kate felt responsible, it was the least she could do. As she drove through Lindale and out along the road to his cottage, she gazed around her at the countryside that had so enchanted her and Louise in the days when they still had time to look. She noticed how beautiful it all was, the bronzed greens of the bush coloured by casuarina russets and the odd splash of early wattle. She would have to leave it all soon, she thought—all this and her dreams of the gallery. And Robert. Especially Robert.

She was greeted delightedly by Philip. 'Come in, my dear. How nice of you to call!' As he glided away from her in the wheelchair, he said, 'Andrew's at work, I'm afraid.'

'I've come to see you, not Andrew, Philip. To give you this.'

She produced the cheque. He handled it curiously and finally looked at her in amazement. 'Do you mean someone has really bought it this time?'

She nodded. Philip was, he told her, 'tickled pink'.

'Well, well,' he kept saying, looking at the cheque. 'This calls for a celebration.' He insisted on fetching them a glass of wine to toast his success and Kate's stomach heaved queasily as she sipped from her glass. After her foolhardiness last night, alcohol was something she could do without today. But she made a pretence of it for Philip's sake.

'You know, Kate, this is very special for me. It gives me a great kick to think that someone has a painting with my signature on it that will still be around when

I'm gone.' She began to protest, but he held up a thin hand. 'No, no I'm not being maudlin. I know I haven't got long, but thanks to Andrew I've already had an extension of time, you might say.' He twinkled at her. 'It's sheer ego to want to have my name perpetuated somewhere, even if it is only on a pretty awful picture that might one day end up on the dump.'

'My customer didn't think it was awful, obviously. In fact she said that it was the only one I had that would do for her.' She tactfully left out the fortunate fact of Mrs Price's purple curtains,

Philip raised his glass. 'You're a very diplomatic girl, Kate. And I appreciate the way you kept my picture for sale after it had been condemned by Robert.' He took her to the back room that was his studio and showed her his latest work. Most of the canvases stacked against the wall were dreadful, but one caught Kate's eye.

'I like that,' she said, giving in to her soft-hearted impulse. 'Would you care to sell it? Same commission as before.'

'You're joking!'

'No. All my artists usually replace sold work with something new.' She made her enterprise sound very grand. 'If you like, I'll arrange to have this framed and hung in place of your other one.'

The look on his face was beatific. Kate left with the canvas, enquiring about Andrew and receiving a shrewd look from Philip. 'Andrew will be sorry to have missed you, Kate.' And she got the feeling that he meant more than just the brief visit.

Why couldn't she have fallen for Andrew? Kate bemoaned on her way home. He was everything a girl could wish for—he was intelligent and sensitive and sweet. She could have been happy with him for a partner instead of shedding tears in the night for

Robert. Angrily she brushed the beginning of new tears from her eyes. She had no one to blame but herself. From the moment she heard his name, she knew she had to forget those revealing moments of her first meeting with Robert. But how hard she had tried. Kate's lips trembled. She had hidden behind insults and a stiff-necked attitude, she had provoked and annoyed him and pretended even to herself that there was nothing about him she liked. While all the time he had built upon that first fatal attraction—built himself a place in her heart that would not be banished in a hurry. If ever.

Blinking hard, Kate drove up the mountain to Galerie Bowman. It was time for her to make new plans, she told herself, pushing aside the self pity that threatened to swamp her. Staying here, seeing Robert— knowing he was near and whisking Sonia Marsden up to his games room would hurt like hell. She thought of the tall blonde in his arms, the way she herself had been last night, and her hands were still clenched on the wheel when she approached the gallery drive and saw the white sports car.

Almost she drove past to postpone the moment when she would have to look on that handsome face again and know that he had used his expertise to teach her a lesson. Thank God she had not actually said, 'I love you'. She would face him—outface him. She gathered her courage and sat for a few moments in the car, staring at the front door before she emerged.

'We'll discuss this tomorrow,' he'd said as if there was anything to discuss. Fleetingly Kate puzzled over that, but girded herself for the sight of him and everything else went out of her head. Now, Kate, she said silently, let's see what kind of an actress you are.

He was talking to Louise in her studio and their voices fell silent as her footsteps went through to the kitchen. Kate flung the curtain aside so that the wooden rings clacked upon each other, and smiled brightly. 'Hello, Mr Beaumont—oh, I forgot, I said I'd call you Robert, didn't I? Not jogging today?' She went on quickly, not waiting for his answer. 'There's a parcel for you in the car from Max, Louise.'

'What were you doing at Max's place? I thought you went to see Philip?'

Kate risked a glance at Robert. He was watching her intently, his grey eyes confused. Had he expected her to be devastated? She held on to her casual offhand manner. If she didn't over-act, he might never know that she was.

'I did, and took another of his paintings for the gallery, then dropped it in to Max's place for framing. I know,' she held up her hands to Robert, 'you're going to say I'm a fool to hang one of his again, but there, I seem to be getting more foolish every day.'

'No, Kate, I wasn't going to say that.'

'That makes a change, then, doesn't it? Anyone for coffee?' God, she thought, this is terrible. She could manage another few minutes, no more.

'Not for me, Kate. I want to see what Max has sent.'

Louise went out to the car and Kate followed her as far as the gallery, heart pounding like a sledgehammer in her chest. The last thing she wanted was to be alone with Robert again.

But she was.

'I want to talk to you, Kate. About last night . . .' he began, then stopped.

She waved a hand and went to straighten a picture that was a millimetre off centre. 'Oh, forget it, Robert. It's just too embarrassing.'

'Embarrassing?' he repeated harshly, and came to take her arm. His touch was nearly her undoing. The fresh, clean smell of him reminded her of dancing in his

arms, of his hands touching her as never before . . .
'You were really very charming and I'd had far too
much to drink. What *did* you put in those lovely tall
concoctions?'

A faint colour stained his cheeks and she felt the
knife turn in her breast. So he had deliberately tried to
make her tipsy. But she couldn't blame the alcohol.
Whatever he had given her had acted like a truth serum.
It had merely released what was already there. And she
had only herself to blame for that.

'So I'm sorry if I rather threw myself at you——' she
wrinkled her brow. 'I remember dancing round and
round in your games room—George Benson was
playing—I remember that, then you——' she looked
down at her hands, 'but I can't recall a great deal after
that.'

'You're a liar, Kate. I made love to you and then I
stopped, and you remember it very well.'

'You stopped!' She put a hand to her breast in
gratitude. 'Oh, I wondered about that—thank you.'

He snorted, and regarded her in exasperation. 'Kate,
this is no good. The reason I stopped isn't what
you . . .'

The telephone rang and Kate hurried to it, a sort of
hysteria creeping up on her. If he didn't go she would
break down and cry, and Robert must never see that.
As she held the handset to her ear, she saw him
watching her with that thwarted look on his face. He
must go before she put the phone down.

'Andrew,' she breathed into the receiver, and there
was dead silence from the other end.

'No, you must be mistaken,' the caller said. 'I just
wanted to know if you have any pottery wine jugs for
sale.'

Kate beamed and looked far away, right through
Robert whose body had stiffened at Andrew's name.

'Lovely, darling. When?'

'Er—wine jugs——?' the man on the phone repeated faintly. 'Would you have any on display?'

'Next weekend? I'm not sure if I could make it next weekend, Andrew. Maybe the one after that.'

Robert sank his hands into his pockets and studied his toecaps.

'—er—are you closed, then, during the week—or—er—this *is* Galerie Bowman, is it?' The caller sounded a little fraught.

'Yes. And so am I, Andy,' Kate cooed, and watched Robert stride to the door. His footsteps clacked on the stairs, then a car door slammed.

'—thought I dialled the right number for Galerie . . .'

Tears welled up in Kate's eyes as she heard the plaintive voice in her ear, then the roar of an engine.

'Galerie Bowman,' she said. 'I believe you're after wine jugs. We've got four in stock right now. We're open every day from ten to five.'

'Thank you. Er—I was talking to a woman there who kept calling me Andrew—sounded a little unhinged.'

'Yes, I think she was. She's gone now.'

'You're losing weight,' Louise said a week later, and looked closely at Kate. 'Is something worrying you?'

'Of course not. Business is bad, our bank balance is low and we have a pile of bills. What's to worry about?'

'I did think,' Louise hesitated, 'you and Robert——'

Kate grinned and ached inside. 'Me and Robert? We're getting along just fine. You should be pleased, Louise. I've managed to overcome my scruples and be quite civil to him. Even you couldn't complain about my behaviour yesterday.'

She had been extremely civil—and she'd made absolutely sure that there was no chance of being alone with Robert again, a fact that he noticed but could do nothing about. Why had he called again, looking at her in that considering way as if—as if what? There was something about it all that didn't quite fit. Why did he keep dropping by—hadn't he achieved his aim? Well, of course he came to see Louise—that was why.

'Robert doesn't seem in very good spirits lately,' Louise remarked.

Kate frowned. That was odd too. Robert had been pleasant and courteous but absent—as if something else was on his mind. Sonia Marsden, perhaps? Or was it possible that he was having regrets about what happened? Regretting maybe that he hadn't taken full advantage of her impulsive offer of herself. Surely that would have been an even greater retribution, if that was what he had wanted. And it couldn't have been easy for him to stop at that point. She reddened. She had been in a position to know that he was as aroused as she was. With a willing partner—why *had* he stopped?

'He looks as if he's grappling with some problem,' her aunt went on, 'but I don't suppose we'll learn what it is.'

'What?' Kate's mind was grappling with her own problems. Why had Robert drawn back when she had agreed to spend the night with him? Painfully she reconstructed the scene again, as she did almost every night—herself lying there with her arms outstretched to him. But each night it made less sense. If he had wanted to teach her a lesson surely he was human enough to take what was offered in the process? In the morning he could have told her that he had planned it that way and the humiliation would have been greater—far greater. Kate worried the question. That night here, when she'd made such a fool of him, he had been furious enough to want to pay her back in like. But since then he had been different. Had all that teasing warmth been turned on merely to trap her into succumbing? 'I intend to win the battle'—but what sort of a general took a small victory when he could have a massive, conclusive one?

The more she thought about it, the more Kate wished she had listened to him when he had called, though what he could possibly say was a mystery.

'Louise,' she found her aunt's eyes on her, 'if he calls again, don't let him go without me seeing him. There's something I want to ask him.'

Louise favoured her with a long, hard look and picked up another mug to glaze. 'I'll do that,' she said placidly.

But Robert didn't come the next day, or the next, and Kate couldn't quite bring herself to drive up to his gallery. She tossed it around in her mind until she could not think clearly at all. 'The reason I stopped isn't what you——' he had begun, and now she burned to know what he would have said. Eventually she *did* drive up to the elegant white building with its vine-hung patio, and Robert was there—with a laughing Sonia Marsden just stepping from her car. He saw the van and Kate gave a cheerful hoot of the horn, then put her foot hard on the accelerator and shot past on her way to nowhere.

CHAPTER NINE

So it was Sonia Marsden on his mind after all. They were practically engaged, so it should be no surprise. Maybe he couldn't make up his mind to give up his freedom and pop the question. That would certainly be a problem for a bachelor to grapple with. All her resentment came back with a vengeance and Kate knew, deep down, that it was in reality pure, unreasoning jealousy.

When Dave Scott rang, chatting ebulliently about his friend Rob, Kate was in a sour mood.

'Hello there, beautiful Kate. I heard you lost the bet,' was his opening remark. Old chum Rob must have kept him informed.

'I wouldn't have thought it important enough for you two to talk about,' she said dryly.

'Since when is dinner with a beautiful girl not a subject for discussion between two red-blooded males?'

Which had Kate wondering just what Robert had told him.

'You'd be surprised at the number of letters we've had from viewers wanting to know what's happening up there between you two,' Scott told her. 'As a matter of fact, that's why I rang. We thought we might come up to film a short piece about your place as a follow-up. What do you think, Kate?'

Her first impulse was to refuse. But the coming exhibition for Evan Gale shot into her mind. He had requested a change of date and she had been forced to fall back on her 'Ransome' pictures to supplement his. Her hastily organised publicity could only be enhanced by exposure on Dave Scott's show.

'As it happens, that would suit me fine,' she said directly. 'We'll be staging our first artists' show shortly and providing you allow me to plug it, I'd be happy for you to film up here.' She mentioned the dates for the Gale/Ransome show and he chuckled.

'And old Rob said you weren't a businesswoman! Fair enough, Kate. Just one thing, though—I'd like Rob to be there too. Are you two getting on any better since that cosy dinner for two?'

Sarcastically she thought, 'Didn't friend Rob tell you that?' Aloud she said, 'Let's say, Dave, that we understand each other now.'

'Well, well—understand, eh? So it's okay with you if Rob is there for the filming?'

What difference could it make? she thought, remembering that first ghastly interview when she had only just managed to hide her tears from the camera. It wouldn't be like that this time. Now she had no wish to score off Robert, and his regard for Louise would prevent him from making any more damaging remarks about Galerie Bowman.

Scott set a time for the following week and promised to let her know if that slot wouldn't suit 'old Rob'.

'Oh, please do,' she said with a touch of unplanned asperity. 'We mustn't inconvenience old Rob.'

'Understand each other, huh?' Dave chuckled. 'Rob isn't an easy guy to understand.' He went on confidingly, 'I've known him for years—I started in the business in Melbourne—and . . .'

It was twenty minutes before she thoughtfully put the phone down.

Louise was amazed that Kate would consider the publicity again after the first unsuccessful occasion. 'This one will be recorded,' Kate told her. 'We can insist on anything unexpected being taken out.' But there wouldn't be anything unexpected. 'Besides, I need the advertising for the Gale/Ransome opening.'

'Will you say *you* are Ransome on the show?' Louise looked suspiciously at her and Kate smiled.

'No. I'm not out for revenge, if that's what you think. Though you have to admit it would be perfect justice.' She could imagine Robert's face if she said that it was *her* to whom he had awarded a distinction, and her picture he had bought. It was a consolation, she supposed, to take through life, that Robert had liked her work. But she could almost wish he hated it—if he could care for her instead.

Kate's clothes were beginning to hang loose. She picked at her food and drank countless cups of coffee to enable her to keep up her pace, then lay awake at night wondering what on earth she would do. Somehow she had to find a way to leave this place without letting Louise down.

Andrew rang, then called to press her to go out with him, and was piqued at her reminders of her busy schedule.

'I heard you honoured that TV bet with Beaumont,' he said. 'Did you have dinner with him too?'

'Yes, I did.'

'Where did you go?' he insisted, jealously. When she didn't immediately answer, he prompted, 'A restaurant?'

'No.'

His boyish face stiffened into defeat. 'Oh, I see. Took you to his place, did he? Cosy!' But he said no more about it, and Kate could think of nothing to say that would make the situation any easier.

'Will you bring me a replacement for your sold painting, Andrew?' she asked as he left.

He turned to look back at her from the steps, his eyes

impossibly blue, his blond hair pale in the sun. 'A replacement?' He gave her a weak smile. 'Yes, cousin Kate, I'll look for one.'

'Will you deliver that consignment to the Lodge for me tomorrow?' Louise asked one night as Kate pored over the accounts.

'Saturday? Will they accept delivery on a weekend?'

'Yes—I checked. And I want you to take the day off. Stay up there in the rain forest and do some drawing. And some eating. You're beginning to look like Twiggy!'

'I'll think about it. There really isn't time for tramping about on bushwalks, Louise.'

But in the morning, her aunt had everything ready— the pottery consignment of jars with their neat-fitting cork seals packed away in the van, and Kate's lunch and sketching gear in an overnight bag.

'What have you put in this?' Kate laughed, and picked up the heavy bag.

'Just your crayons, pens, charcoal, watercolours, pads, thermos flask, sandwiches——'

'Okay, okay! I'm equipped for the day, I see. Thanks, Louise.'

Her aunt hurried away to answer the telephone as Kate went out and she knew it was Max from the eager tone of Louise's voice.

She was almost to the car when she saw Robert's familiar figure jogging up the road's slope and she willed him to pass on by. But he slowed as she opened the passenger door of the van and hoisted the bag on to the seat. When she slammed the door shut he came over to her.

'Hello, Robert,' she said casually, and hoped her slamming heart wasn't as loud from where he stood. Broodingly he searched her face, looked at her too-trim figure in the skirt and sweater that fitted better than most. She had taken extra trouble with her appearance this morning in an effort to allay Louise's worry about her health. Her make-up gave her a fresh, rested look and disguised the shadows under her eyes. She had brushed her glowing hair until it shone and curved softly about her face. His eyes slipped to the van window and he looked in at the bag on the seat.

'So you are going. I didn't think you would.'

Kate's gaze followed his. What was he talking about?

'I suppose the fact that I told you he wasn't right for you made you determined to do it anyway. You're so damned immature you shouldn't be out by yourself.'

Her hackles rose at his tone. He thought she was going away with Andrew, and she could easily enlighten him. But her heart thumped crazily and her tongue ran away on its defensive tack.

'But I won't be alone, will I, Robert? Anyway, you're doing Andrew an injustice if you think I'd encourage him just to defy you.'

His mouth twisted. Kate noticed that he was rather pale considering he had been jogging, but her own face flamed as he went on.

'You used him before to hide behind because you haven't the courage to face your feelings for me.'

'What feelings? You arrogant, conceited . . .!'

He reached out and took her arm, pulled it so sharply that she was thrown against him. Angrily he looked down at her and so close she could see the tumult in his grey eyes.

'Have a nice weekend, Kate,' he grated, and kissed her crushingly, bending her head back with the force of it. All his anger was in it, but even so Kate felt the weakness begin to take her. He was not asking for response and released her at the moment she began to give it. Without another word or a look, he spun around and resumed his running.

Trembling, she waited a minute, then drove slowly away, catching a glimpse of Louise in the doorway as she turned the van in the same direction as Robert. It crossed her mind that her aunt might have seen them, but as her gaze settled on the dark blue track-suited figure ahead, it didn't seem to matter much. She fumbled for her sunglasses and was wearing them as she passed him on the road, which was just as well, because she was crying. As she neared the next bend, she saw his broad-shouldered figure in the side mirror, then there was nothing but the blurred outline of another car and trees until she passed Beaumont Galleries.

Her stupid temper had got in the way again. She could so easily have told him where she was going instead of allowing his attitude to goad her into more lies. He had sounded almost jealous. Perhaps, after all—but there was Sonia. Kate sighed and took the turn-off that led high up into the range.

Day trippers disembarked from a mini-bus at the Lodge, hung with their cameras and binoculars and bags. Guests leaving stood with their luggage on the verandah, their eyes far away and regretful. Those arriving banged down the boots of cars and strode eagerly to the office. Kate saw Louise's pottery safely inside, briefly chatted with the harassed office manager and left, turning in the direction of the nearest National Park entrance. Within minutes she was stationary and overlooking the endless peaks and valleys that stretched down to the New South Wales border. For a few minutes she sat in the car, letting her eyes follow the tree-covered ridges as they dropped into emerald and indigo valleys to rise again into the gold touch of the sun. The jagged outlines of the mountains retreated in tone until they cut the horizon in misted mauve-blues and greys. And above it all was the blue and cloudless sky. 'I fell in love with the mountains,' Robert had said.

Everything came back to Robert, she thought resignedly, and her focus slipped from the magnificent mountains. She thought of him driving Sonia Marsden up to his beautiful house, smiling down at her as she elegantly slipped from her car at his gallery, remembered the proprietorial hold Sonia had kept on him at Clarry's party. Until he had slipped away and danced with her and almost propositioned her. Would Robert have done that if he was on the brink of a permanent relationship with Sonia? She frowned. It didn't seem the kind of behaviour that typified him. He had principles— Evan Gale insisted on that, and even Dave Scott had shed his usual flippancy when he had phoned a week earlier, to put in a good word for Robert. Though why he should have done so puzzled her.

'He's the straightest guy I know,' Dave told her, 'absolutely down the line with everyone from a Dobell to a dabbler. And that goes for his private life too.'

'You don't have to play advocate for him to me, Dave,' she had said, and hadn't been able to resist a little fishing. 'He doesn't care what I think of him. He might welcome your championing him with Sonia Marsden, though.'

'Ah yes, the curvaceous Sonia.' He laughed. 'Not a match. He won't marry her. He had his fingers burned once and he won't make a mistake like that.'

'Do you mean Dyan?'

'Told you about that, did he? He wanted to marry her but she put a career above anything. It paid off too. She can name her price for her work now. Lives in the Greek Islands. I'm surprised he mentioned her. That must have been a *very* cosy dinner!'

'I learned a few things,' she admitted dryly.

'Is that so? Well, Kate, just bear in mind that Rob has a few vulnerable spots . . .'

Vulnerable. It was hard to believe Robert was that, and yet this morning he had looked shaken, even hurt, though he had tried to disguise it in anger.

Kate left the car, hitching her bag over one shoulder, and set off to the nearest walking track. A sign showed a map of a circular route which led to a waterfall and back again. Circular routes seemed to be her speciality, she mused—all that resistance, that struggling against her feeling for Robert had brought her full circle to her initial fascination. All paths led back to him. The question was—in which direction was *he* going?

The path was steep and rough, winding and turning back upon itself. It was rocky and studded with tree roots so that she kept her eyes to the ground, only partly aware of the changing vegetation as she descended. As the track flattened out at last, she walked from the sun specked open into the shade of the rain forest. It always surprised her—the suddenness of it. The edge of the forest was as clearly defined as a wall. It *was* a wall—of green tangled leaves and branches, and the path she trod was a tunnel into its other world.

The heavy weight in her chest seemed more burdensome in here. As she slowed her pace to look up along the slender stems of palms and the massive columns of cedar and rosewood, she felt a pang that had nothing to do with the majesty of the forest. What it would be to walk in here with Robert, no barriers between them. Just the two of them? 'Fool!' she whispered fiercely, and somewhere high, parrots shrieked in the canopy that was supported by the great arches of branches. Lianas spiralled about buttressed trunks and slender saplings, like some ornamental carving. Orchids and staghorn ferns grew lush and green high above where the light filtered down in cathedral gloom as through some giant stained glass windows.

Kate stopped and breathed in the hush and the

warm, rich odour of humus. Now she could hear the muted roar of the waterfall and the first notes of the whip-bird's ritual cry. She closed her eyes and tried to make the forest's peace hers, and in a little while it worked. Not entirely, but she felt some of her misery slip away. It wasn't possible to remain hopeless in here, she thought. To bring them here was like taking your troubles to church. With the peace came the calm decision to break down the barriers between herself and Robert. Or to try.

The waterfall was a mere shadow of itself, for the winter so far had been dryer than usual. But still it leaped in white and silver over the rock precipice that channelled it on its way downwards and left its spray on quivering palm spears and trembling lacy fern fronds. Kate sat for half an hour just watching and thinking, then withdrew her lunch and her sketchbook and sat for another hour. But the drawings she made bore little resemblance to the scenery. Full face and profile sketches found their way into the pages of wild rain forest growth. Sketches of a strong-jawed face with straight brows and an aristocratic nose.

Later, as she turned into the drive of Galerie Bowman, she was aware of uncertainty returning—like some bird of prey settling down to wait. The clarity of the rain forest was lost to her, and she grew thinner while she matched need with pride and waited on the outcome.

In the end, the decision to see Robert was taken out of her hands. He did not call at the gallery, at least not while she was there, and Kate watched the road in vain. She even tended the garden early each morning, but he had apparently stopped his morning jog past them, because she didn't see him. Preoccupied with the problem, she thought she was hearing things when Louise calmly asked her to run an errand to Robert's house.

'To pick up that jug of mine he bought. He wants me to make a similar one for his mother.'

'Jug?' Kate repeated stupidly, picturing it elegantly displayed on the shelves in the big room with the rock wall.

'He said he would drop it in—figuratively speaking—tomorrow, but I want to start work on it this morning. Be a love and run up for it, will you?'

Kate saw her chance. She went to change out of her work clothes and carefully applied make-up and swept her hair up with combs. Louise eyed her pants suit and said blandly, 'You look very nice.'

As she drove away, Kate thought it was possible that Louise had seen her in Robert's arms that morning. But she hadn't mentioned it.

The gallery was shut and Kate swept on up the long drive to his house, remembering another time when she had traversed it, jangling with a different kind of nerves.

A woman answered the door and introduced herself as the housekeeper. 'I think Mr Beaumont has it all ready in his den,' she told her.

Kate followed the woman, her heart sinking. Did that mean he wasn't there? She hadn't thought of that. 'Just along there, Miss Bowman. Will you excuse me? I've got something on the stove.'

Kate hesitated at the closed door to the games room, then passed by to a study. There was no one there, but the jug was on the desk, swathed in tissue and nestled in a box. She lingered to look at the traces of Robert in the room. A pile of papers lay there, covered in the same bold hand that had written her name in his diary. A pen was beside the notes, and a pair of cufflinks. She could imagine him starting his work, removing the links to roll up his sleeves.

Dispiritedly, she took the parcel and went, hesitating

again at the closed door in the corridor. On impulse she pushed it open and walked in, swallowing on the painful memories it evoked—painful or magic, depending on the point in time. Up until that moment when she had held her arms up to him, it was magic—but then she had seen his hesitation—was that the word? Kate frowned, closed her eyes to bring the moment into focus. Robert had looked down at her and she had read petty vengeance in his eyes. But his breathing was rapid—as rapid as hers, and he had been about to speak. What would he have said, had she not so quickly interpreted his silence?

Kate opened her eyes on the life-size nude above the bar.

'Kate.'

She almost dropped Louise's jug and whirled around as Robert came in. He was dressed formally in a three-piece suit which mellowed the athletic shape of him into elegance. As he drew closer, bringing with him the atmosphere that only he created, Kate tried to think of a way to say what she wanted.

'I came for the jug,' she said inanely, indicating the package under her arm.

'Why did you come into this room?'

'I—just wanted to look at—one of the pictures.'

'I see,' he nodded, and she felt her opportunity slipping away. Pride would have to give way to need.

They both spoke at once.

'Robert, about last week—I didn't go away with . . .'

'Kate, about that night here—the reason I didn't . . .'

Silence fell. They both smiled nervously, then stared at each other. Kate's eyes widened at what she saw in Robert's and they were posed on the brink of understanding, the space between them dissolving when the door opened again.

'Rob—oh! I didn't realise you had—a visitor.' Sonia

Marsden came in and draped herself on Robert. Her fingers curled smugly under his sleeve and emerged red-tipped and possessive in the crook of his arm. 'Sorry I'm late, darling,' she said with a studiedly uninterested look at Kate. 'You know how I hate getting out of bed in the mornings.'

'Sonia, Kate and I have business to discuss—if you wouldn't mind . . .?'

The blonde girl shrugged, pouted. 'Of course, darling.'

Kate smiled brightly. 'It doesn't matter. It's not as if I had an appointment.'

She started to move, like a brisk businesswoman with somewhere to go, something urgent to do.

'Kate——'

'Goodbye, Miss Marsden, Robert.' She opened the door and looked back. 'It was nothing important.'

Quickly she walked to the front door and let herself out, carefully laid the jug on the back seat and drove home.

'Here you are, Louise—all in one piece.' Which was more than she could say for herself. Louise studied her.

'Did you see Robert?'

'Yes, I saw him.'

She changed into her oldest clothes and fetched a machete from the lean-to. Then she trekked into the longest, thickest grass in the back garden and hacked and threshed until her tears dried and fallen stems lay all about her.

On the day that Dave Scott was coming to film his segment, Kate woke more pale and strained than ever. Her head ached and her throat was scratchy. The prospect of seeing Robert again today made the pounding in her ears worse, and she took some aspirin knowing that it would ease only part of the pain.

'You look ghastly,' Louise told her.

'Gee, thanks.' Kate swallowed some toast and tea and went to disguise her pallor with make-up. Only her hair, she thought vaguely, had any life at all. Its copper sheen was undiminished and it waved around her face in the nearest thing to animation she had.

Dave's eyes lingered on it when he arrived. 'Ah, beautiful Kate,' he said, taking her hands. But the shrewd eyes moved on to notice the smudges under hers and the smooth hollows of her cheeks.

While the cameraman investigated the lighting Dave used his easy manner to relax Kate. An impossible task, she would have thought, listening for the throaty sound of a sports car in the drive, but she did unwind a little. Dave had a special kind of exhibitionist charm and he kept her laughing—almost laughing, even as a door slammed shut outside and footsteps sounded on the steps.

When Robert came in, the laugh died on her lips. He registered the change sourly.

'You must be in good form today Dave,' he said dryly to the compère, and didn't seem too impressed with Dave's man-to-man nudge.

'I'm always in good form when it comes to chatting up gorgeous girls,' said Dave, grinning at the taller man.

'So your wife tells me,' Robert replied with a taut smile. There was a startled silence and Dave looked speculatively from his friend to Kate. A soundless whistle pursed his lips before he turned to organise the filming. Lights were switched on and the cameraman stood ready with a hand camera and a battery pack around his waist.

'This might end up being a five-minute job when you see it,' Dave explained. 'But we'll play it by ear and take the best bits to go to air. Okay?'

'As long as you leave in my plug for the two-man show,' Kate reminded him.

'Oh, sure.'

There was a quality of déjà-vu about the scene as Dave introduced them again and picked up the story from the foolish bet made by Kate on his programme.

'We know you lost the bet, Kate, and paid up by working at Robert's place for a day. Has that changed your views?'

What would he think if she told him just how much it had changed them? 'Not about art,' she replied unwarily.

'Now *that's* interesting. About Rob himself, perhaps?' Dave grinned hopefully.

'I think I understand his point of view better. But I don't agree with it.'

Dave looked disappointed. He would prefer fireworks or a nice solid romance to please his viewers and he was getting cold porridge. The interview continued low-key. Kate pointed out that Philip's picture had in fact been sold, although she had lost the bet, and with a flash of her old defiance she indicated the new piece of his work hanging.

'Care to comment on this one Rob?' queried Dave, and Kate stiffened. Robert didn't even look at it.

'Philip hasn't forgiven me for my last criticism yet, and since then I've regretted being so harsh. I will always deplore the fact that people try to sell art of this standard, but Kate tells me that many people can enjoy it on their journey to a higher appreciation.' He looked at Kate as he spoke and some small spark of hope fluttered in her. It was a handsome admission from Robert—as handsome as she could expect, knowing his stringent adherence to excellence.

'And I'd be happy to discuss that—and other matters—with Miss Bowman over dinner again,' he added, to Dave's delight—and hers. Perhaps after all—she began to be impatient for the filming to

finish so that they could talk and this time it would
be different.

Dave was speaking directly to the camera. 'And
Galerie Bowman will be showing works by Evan Gale
and B. Ransome—what's the "B" stand for, Kate?'

'I don't know,' she said lamely, and saw Robert
stiffen, his eyes narrow.

'Well, I guess it doesn't matter—come on up and
enjoy the scenery everyone and pop into Kate's place.
The show starts on . . .'

The compère finished his very generous plug for
Kate's showing and wound up the segment, plainly
disappointed that it had gone so tamely. But he was all
ears when Robert looked Kate over sardonically and
virtually accused her of tracking down Ransome just to
spite him.

'Were you so desperate to notch up a victory over
me, Kate?' he sounded less angry than weary, but his
disgust with her was plain.

She didn't even bother to defend herself. 'It's no
victory, Robert, believe me.' The small spark of hope
went out. There would be no question of Robert talking
to her over dinner or anywhere else now. She was tired
and desolate. Suddenly she didn't give a damn about
the gallery, Evan's exhibition, Louise's pottery or
anything. Her head pounded and her throat was on fire
and all she wanted to do was to crawl away somewhere
and fall into the oblivion of sleep. She hardly even
noticed when Robert left, except to register the starting
roar of his car.

Later, Kate couldn't have said how she managed to
get through the next half hour when Dave and the
cameraman sat down to drink coffee and talk in the
bright and brittle manner of the industry. At last Dave
saw the effort in Kate's face and made a move to leave.
It was Louise who saw them out. When they had gone

she turned anxiously to Kate, who was standing quite still in the gallery staring at the floor.

'Kate, what is it?' Louise peered at her face, curtained by the fiery hair.

'My head aches, Lou, and my throat's sore—I must have picked up a virus . . .'

She spoke as if she was in a dream, and Louise's concern grew.

'My dear, is that all that's bothering you?' She put a hand on Kate's shoulder and it was enough to release the tide.

'Lou, I'm so miserable!' she cried, and turned her face into her aunt's shoulder as if she was a child again.

'I know, Katie, I know,' soothed Louise and cradled her.

'It's my temper—my rotten temper. If I'd only once . . .'

Louise led her to the bedroom. 'Get into bed, Kate. I'll bring you some aspirin and tea.'

When she had gone Kate gave a desperate sort of giggle. Aspirin and tea! If only that was the cure she needed! She undressed and slipped under the covers and giggled again until she cried. The pillow was cool, so cool, and it changed under Kate's fingers to white patterned with red and black. She caressed Robert's silk shirt as he whirled her about a large room, then cried out as Louise came back to stand beside the bed. With a start she came back to reality. 'Did I say something?' she asked Louise, bewildered.

'You called "Robert",' her aunt said gently.

'He thinks I got hold of Ransomes pictures just to spite him,' she gabbled, the words beginning to fall over themselves as the fever built. 'But I meant to tell him it was me——' Tears welled up in the confused green eyes and Louise laid a cool hand on the damp forehead, deciding that tea and aspirin weren't the answer to any of Kate's problems.

'Why didn't you tell him just now, Kate?'

'Dave Scott was there . . . make him look a fool. And I don't want to fight with him any more . . .'

Louise waited a few more moments and Kate mumbled, 'He wanted me to stay till morning, Lou—and I said yes.'

Tenderly Louise smoothed her heated brow and Kate's childishly perplexed eyes closed as she fell into an uneasy sleep.

'Stay until morning . . .' murmured Kate, and Louise went to phone the doctor.

For two days Kate tossed in the grip of the fever induced by the virus. On the third day she lay, cool and rational and as weak as Vincent had been when Max found him on the road. When the doctor called again he stressed that it would be a few days before she could work again, and Kate fretted that Louise would fall behind with her orders if she had no help. But the calm voice of her aunt overrode her protests.

'Rest. Max will take over the gallery for a few days.'

'But Evan Gale—the exhibition—I've got to do all——'

'Leave it to us,' Louise's quiet voice came back. 'Max and I will attend to everything.'

And they did. There was nothing for Kate to do but to rest, pale and wan between her flowered sheets, her hand stroking Vincent's purring body—and think.

CHAPTER TEN

KATE finished her painting of the back garden, baffling Max by admitting she was Ransome.

'What does the "B" stand for?' he asked, and she laughed and shrugged. 'I don't know.'

But Max's other questions remained unasked and his shrewd brown eyes held disconcerting understanding. She began the portrait of Max, working from sketches he reluctantly posed for, and sent out invitations to the Gale/Ransome opening. With care she wrote Robert's name on one, forlornly following it with 'and friend'. He was away, Louise told her. Indefinitely. He probably wouldn't come even if he was home in time.

It was spring at last, and the mornings came sooner and warmed more quickly. The bronze and pink of new tender growth tinged the bushland that lined the mountain road and the small jungle in their back yard. Kate's flowers were in bud in the rock garden and one or two miniature marigolds were blooming already. The bedding begonias had never recovered from the late winter frost and were browned and ragged. 'I know how you feel,' Kate told them, and looked along the sloping road to Beaumont Galleries.

On the opening night, Kate and Louise surveyed the gallery. Evan's paintings, large and vigorous, glowed under the extra lighting fixed up by Max. Kate's pictures were modestly scattered, their size diminutive in comparison but effective. A couple of Louise's free-form vases stood on the floor filled with honesty and trembling wild grasses. Trays of wine glasses waited on the champagne and the guests. Max's last chore before going home to change was to fill their laundry tubs with ice and bottles.

'We owe Max a great deal,' Kate murmured to her aunt.

'He's happy to do it.' Louise smiled, and something in the way her aunt looked down at her clasped hands alerted Kate. She reached out and uncovered Louise's work-roughened left hand. On the third finger gleamed a modest diamond. For the first time in weeks, Kate's eyes glowed with life. She threw her arms about Louise and hugged her.

'Congratulations, you sly thing! How long have you had that on? Did he propose to you over the ice in the laundry this afternoon?'

'Nothing so impetuous,' her aunt replied serenely.

Kate flew to the laundry and came back with a bottle of champagne. The cork launched into the gallery and skittered on the floor, closely followed by Vincent. The wine chuckled into two glasses and Kate lifted hers in a toast. 'To you and Max, my darling aunt. The perfect match.'

They stood, Louise in curlers and both wearing their dressing gowns, and drank several more toasts recklessly proposed by Kate.

'That's enough, Kate.' Louise put her glass down firmly. 'Otherwise our guests may arrive to find their hostesses staggering!'

They went to the bedroom, arm in arm, to dress for the occasion.

'Black was probably the wrong choice for me at present,' said Kate, eyeing the effect of her pallor against the dark fabric. But make-up and a liberal application of blusher remedied that, and her hair fell in undimmed radiance to brush the bare skin of her neck exposed by the deep neckline of the dress. She joked with Louise about her forthcoming marriage with a smile on her lips, while at the back of her mind lurked the question. What would she do now? She had been looking for a way to leave this place without letting Louise down, and now that it had been handed to her she shrank from it. A little more thoughtful, she applied green eyeshadow to her lids and disguised the shadows under her eyes. If only, she thought, everything was so easy to disguise.

'By the way,' Louise said after a while, 'Max told me that Robert came back today.'

Concentrating fiercely on applying mascara, Kate murmured, 'Oh yes?' but her heart was pumping furiously and her hand shook so that a speck of black smeared her cheek.

'Damn!' she muttered.

'I just thought I'd mention it, in case he decided to come after all.'

'He won't—not now. He's mad because he thinks I deliberately raced him to Ransome.'

'As far as I can see, Kate, Robert has had cause to be angry with you from the start—but he has always come back. Didn't you ever think it odd that he started dropping by after the TV show?' Louise smiled at Kate's wide eyes. 'I did predict it, you know—that Robert Beaumont would carry you off when he saw you. And if you'd just stopped arguing long enough he would have done so by now.'

'But how can I be sure . . .' Kate's doubt clouded her eyes.

'There are no guarantees, Kate. You can't run away for ever because Dan—your father—struck out in love. Give Robert a chance if he comes tonight.'

Louise patted her hair and smoothed her dress, drawing her hand slowly down one hip so that her ring caught the light. Her expression was sheepish as she saw Kate watching her, but she merely said as she left the room, 'Remember, Kate, if you see Robert tonight—civility!' Her eyes smiled with affection and understanding. 'Though I'm sure Robert wants more from you than that! But it could be a start.'

Louise answered the door to Max and Kate let them have a few minutes alone. If Robert *did* come tonight ... she put her hands to her face, suddenly afraid and delighted at the prospect. She would be pleasant, she resolved.

'Pleasant!' She said it out loud, aware of the irony. To Robert she would like to be much more than pleasant. With a touch of her old sparkle, she joined her aunt and Max in the gallery. She planted a congratulatory kiss on Max's whiskered cheek.

'I know you'll be very happy,' she said. 'This old place will become *the* place to buy pottery.' She went on brightly, letting them know in her own way that, whatever happened, she wouldn't be hanging about playing gooseberry.

Then the first guest arrived, to be greeted by Louise while Max opened the first bottle of champagne and Kate produced a tray of savouries. Evan Gale arrived with his wife, a tall, awkward woman dressed in flowing Indian cotton, and they were quickly followed by a number of people unknown to Kate. Andrew arrived with reserve in his blue eyes and the pretty brunette, Rachel, on his arm. Philip Barrett was with them and waved his cheque at Kate.

'I'll keep this to look at a bit longer, Kate,' he told her. 'It's my first and maybe *only* gallery sale.' She laughed and hid a stab of sadness at the old man's exuberance. Thank goodness for Mrs Price and her purple curtains, she thought.

'Who knows,' she said as she passed the tray of hors d'oeuvres to each of them, 'your other one might sell too.'

Philip Barrett took her hand. 'You should have been
diplomat, Kate my dear. Good luck with your
xhibition.'

She smiled, responded, poured champagne and
assed out catalogues, watching for one imperious
rofile among the visitors. Clarry Henderson came in
without Kate seeing him and appeared before her, big
nd bluff and hearty.

'Very nice, my dear. I've seen Evan's stuff before, but
don't recall any of this Ransome fellow's. Not at all
ad. I've got my eye on that cityscape over there.' He
ointed with his champagne glass. 'Fancy that for my
tudy.'

Kate blushed and was about to admit it was her
ork, but the genial man saw an acquaintance and
xcused himself with a promise to see her when he'd
ade up his mind.

'Get your stickers ready,' he called over his shoulder,
nd Kate warmed to him. Maybe his obvious keenness
o buy would start the ball rolling. His wife smiled
erfunctorily at Kate when she refilled her glass. 'Very
ice,' she said.

Kate wandered among the guests, curious to see what
as taking their attention. Evan Gale and his wife had
lit up in an experienced division of duty to fill in
etails on some of his paintings for interested viewers.

'Evan is passionately concerned with conservation . . .'
e heard Mrs Gale say, 'and it shows here, where
e . . .'

Louise's head bobbed up behind someone and she
emed to be saying something but Kate couldn't hear.
'll see you in a moment,' she mouthed, and went to
tch another bottle of champagne from the laundry
bs. Out at the back of the house it was quiet and the
uzz of voices punctuated by laughter, was a distant,
uted thing. Robert had not come and Kate longed for

it to be over so that she could put away the brigh
charming personality she had assumed. But she reache
the doorway and slipped through the curtain to th
growing crowd of guests, donning her hostess's smile.

Dave Scott received the full benefit of it and greete
her in full show-business style with his arms about he
waist and an enthusiastic kiss on the cheek. Kate shoo
her head at him and he grinned irrepressibly back.
she hadn't turned he would have kissed her just a
soundly on the mouth.

'I'm glad you could come, Dave. You're our one an
only celebrity.'

He took the bottle from her, grabbed some glasse
from a near-by bench and filled them expertly. 'As
said, Kate my love, you're a real businesswoman.' Sh
put her head on one side. 'You really don't mind m
using you? I couldn't have got a photographer he
otherwise.'

Wickedly he surveyed her, brown eyes glinting behir
his glasses. 'Using me? Kate, that sounds qui
indecent.' He turned and passed a glass of champagr
to a woman behind him, drawing her forward. 'Mee
my wife Denise—this is Kate Bowman, Dee.'

Kate was visibly embarrassed, remembering h
affectionate greeting, but the tiny blonde woman hel
out her hand and smiled.

'Don't worry, Kate,' Dave laughed at her discomfo
'my wife understands me. You've no idea what
burden it is!'

Louise squeezed by and said one word in Kate's ea
'Civility.' It was enough to give her warning. But tha
didn't stop her heart picking up speed when she turne
to find Robert's eyes on her as he shook hands wi
Dave. Her spirits rose, only to nosedive again as Son
Marsden's sleek figure joined Robert, and though sh
didn't clutch his arm in triumphant possession th

time, she might just as well have done. For Sonia looked rather pleased with herself. Kate's hand shook and a few drops of champagne splashed from her glass down her black dress. Her hostess's smile was stitched firmly on, but it frayed a little under the impact of Robert's cool grey eyes. He was strikingly dressed in dark trousers and jacket over a cream open necked shirt. A gold chain glinted near his collar and a hint of dark chest hair. Tension tightened the cords of his neck and squared his jaw.

'Your opening is off to a good start,' he said dryly. 'I noticed Louise marking a picture sold already.'

'Yes—we hope it will work out.' Kate wrenched her eyes from him to see Sonia looking about with decided pleasure in her eyes. It wasn't for the pictures either, Kate thought, which only left one other reason she could think of. She smiled embracingly at them all. How very civil she was being, all things considered.

'I do hope you all enjoy the evening,' she began to move.

'I've seen Evan—did you manage to get Ransome to come as well?' Robert's voice was sarcastic, and Kate was flustered.

'Well—yes—and no.' She went quickly, 'Excuse me.'

As their first—and probably last—opening it was going well. Clarry had indeed bought the painting he had picked out for his study, and one of Evan's had gone as well. Just the sale of those two would do much to offset the expenditure of the show, and Kate tried hard to feel elated. He head was full of cotton wool as she poured, smiled, fetched new catalogues, smiled—until it was like a bad dream.

Dave was holding court among the crowd. She heard him say, 'And when I was invited to the Gale–Ransome show, I thought it was a striptease act, so naturally I came like a shot ...' Among his audience was Sonia

Marsden and a tall young man who had his arm around
her waist. Kate looked rapidly about, wondering if
Robert knew that his girl-friend was so friendly with
another man. She saw Robert walking alone around the
paintings, no doubt in his own world of the critic.
Carefully she avoided him, but her eyes returned again
and again to his dark head as it appeared through the
throng. After a while she didn't see him at all and didn't
know whether to be glad or sorry that he might have
slipped away. But Sonia remained, and Kate frowned as
she saw the blonde's long, narrow hand on the young
man's arm.

What was going on? she thought, while she smiled
and endeavoured to keep up her end of a discussion on
post-painterly abstraction with an earnest couple.
Where was Robert, and why was Sonia with another
man? The last question remained unanswered, but the
first was solved when she tore herself away from her
guests to face Robert. Unsmiling, he took her arm in a
vicelike grip and steered her to the end of the gallery.

'Let me go!' she hissed through smiling lips and threw
an 'I'll be with you in a moment' look to a guest who
moved towards her with a question on his face. Robert
swung her to a standstill and she almost lost her
balance. Her promise to be pleasant to him shattered.

'How dare you . . .' she began, and her words died as
she looked at the painting in front of them, one that
was holding Robert's sternest gaze. It was the one she
had finished while recovering from the virus, and it had
turned out rather well. The back garden, a section of
the house, and in the long grass, parted to create a
shadow, she had painted Vincent. But Robert obviously
didn't care for this example of Ransome's work.

'Do you want to buy it?' she asked flippantly, and
met his narrowed eyes before the realisation hit her. She
looked back to the cat, distinctively tawny among the

local grasses and trees. And the brown-stained house. Of course he would recognise it. Her green eyes flew back to his face and he took her arm again in a tight grip.

'I want to talk to you—and I don't mean here.' With a steel hold on her, he steered her through the people, passing the group where his girl-friend stood with another man, listening to Dave Scott, and to the front door. The compère's brown eyes followed the two heads, one dark and the other gleaming copper until they reached the door. With a faint nod Dave watched them disappear. Louise too watched them go and made her way to Max.

'Should I have said anything, Max?' She bit her lip.

'You said just enough,' he assured her.

The guests finished off the savouries, had another round of drinks. A red sticker was affixed to another Gale picture and someone made an offer on the pottery vase full of dried grasses. The gallery was crowded with champagne-humoured people and the hum of voices rose to send a tawny-coloured cat slinking outside for some peace and quiet.

The white sports car performed a tight circle and shot up the hill as another car pulled up.

'That's the photographer arriving,' Kate exclaimed. 'You can't just drive me away . . .'

'Can't I?'

Kate held her arm, massaging the marks of his fingers. 'Who do you think you are? You are the most overbearing, arrogant man I've ever met! That's *my* gallery you're dragging me from and *my* guests who are going to . . .'

'Shut up, Kate.' The words snapped out with such authority that she was momentarily silenced. They were halfway up his drive and headed for his house. Alarm triggered off her tongue again. Alarm and a crazy hope.

But there was Sonia back there in the gallery. Kate was hopelessly confused.

'This is kidnapping! You dragged me into your car without so much as a . . .'

'Be quiet!'

'. . . and you hurt me!'

The car stopped and he was around and opening the door before she could reach for the handle. He hauled her out and took her arm again.

'Oh!' she cried. 'Robert, you're hurting me!'

He stopped then and loosened his hold. 'I'm sorry,' he said abruptly, and opened the door for her to enter. Kate saw his face again in the light of the foyer and she quailed at the anger in him. For the first time that night she noticed that the grooves on each side of his mouth were more marked and that he looked tired. He was exercising some strong restraint, evident in the tensed muscle in one cheek and the jutting of his jaw. She walked past him and on into the beautiful living area, hoping that he would not unleash all his pent-up anger on her. Her own nerves were ragged and she could easily cry like a baby.

She stood irresolute on the thick carpet, her spirit flagging now that she was here where she had never thought to be again. The brief flare of temper in the car had left her weary. She looked around at the barely lit room, her gaze lingering on the wall built of rock and an empty angled wall space that jarred somehow, but she couldn't think why. After the noise and smoky atmosphere of the gallery, this house was dead silent, pristine in its uncluttered perfection.

Robert threw his car keys down with a clatter and stared at her, hands on hips in an arrogant pose.

'B. Ransome, I presume,' he said finally.

'Yes.'

He sank his hands into his pockets and stalked about the room frowning, to stop in front of her.

'You must have had a laugh when I gave you a Highly Commended!'

Kate summoned up a smile. 'Oh yes, I had a laugh at that.'

The grey eyes narrowed. 'And then when I bought it for the gallery—quite a triumph for you.'

She flashed him a speaking look. 'Yes, wasn't it?' But a brief one. His own triumph had cast hers in the shade.

'You hid it well. If Louise hadn't advised me to look a little closer at the picture tonight, I might not have known even now. Did you intend to tell me?'

'One day, I suppose.' She gave a brittle laugh. 'I was busy planning how I could use my success to make you squirm the way you did to me and Philip.'

Robert paced about the room again and went to the bar and poured two drinks. He brought one over to her and she looked at it, then at him without taking it. Impatiently he thrust it at her.

'Oh, for God's sake, Kate, take the bloody thing!'

Her eyes widened and she took it, moving warily to the settee.

'Why didn't you say you were Ransome when we did the segment for Dave? You could have made me look a fool then.'

'I couldn't be bothered. Actually Robert, I found that it didn't mean a great deal to me that you liked my picture, or bought it.' She raised her shoulders in a careless shrug. 'At first I thought it might be fun to tell everyone that you had one of my paintings actually hanging in your gallery, but—well, I found myself occupied with more pleasant things.'

'You mean Barrett?' he grated.

Kate just smiled.

'He wasn't paying you much attention tonight. He was all eyes for that brunette with him.'

'She's Philip's nurse.' The lie sprang readily to her

lips. 'And Andrew knew I was too busy to spend time with him tonight. However——' she left the statement hanging.

'I don't believe you're involved with him.'

'Really, Robert, whether or not you believe it is of no consequence. And now,' she stood up, 'if you have nothing to say to excuse your arrogance in dragging me away from my guests, would you please drive me back? Or are you planning a repeat of that other night here first?' She glanced at her full glass on the table. 'But I refuse to get conveniently drunk for you tonight.'

Anger thinned his mouth and etched the frown deeper on to his brow.

'It wasn't only the drink that made you want to stay with me, Kate, and you know it.'

She was more than a little angry herself now and failed to hear the uncertainty in his voice.

'No, it wasn't just the drink. It was the whole expert setting. You really know how to set the scene for seduction, don't you, Robert?' She waved her hand around the room. 'All that piped music and lights that mysteriously kept getting lower and just a dash of comedy to stop the victim getting suspicious. Games Room!' she said scathingly, knowing she should stop by the blackness of his face. 'All those pin-ball machines and billiards are just for show. The *real* games take place on the velvet couches!'

'Victim?' The word unrolled menacingly and Kate took a step back.

'Yes, victim. I'm afraid my experience hasn't equipped me to deal with a determined Don Juan.' She took another step back and another as Robert came for her.

'You sharp-tongued little ...' he bit the words off roughly and quickened his stride. A retort hovered on Kate's tongue, but she lost her courage and turned tail, skirting behind the settee and down the two carpeted steps into the dining room. His hand touched her arm and she was spurred on by panic, trying to remember the location of the front door and drawing a complete blank. She hesitated and was lost. Robert's hands closed over her shoulders, pulling her to a stop so abruptly that her hair swung across her face. She was spun around to face him with strands of copper red across her eyes.

'You don't know how lucky you were, Kate my dear,' he said in an ominous purr. 'A really determined Don Juan would have taken your very generous offer.' He bent and lifted her, ignoring her kicking and struggling and began to walk. 'But let's pick up where we left off, shall we?'

'Robert, let me down—what are you——' Her flailings increased when he turned into the hall to the games room. He turned his back and burst through the swing doors with her and switched on one light with his elbow. The doors flapped to and fro behind them.

'Let me—oh!' The breath left her body as he tossed her unceremoniously on to one of the red-covered couches. She tried to leap up immediately, but he barred her way. Slowly, his eyes never leaving hers, he began to shed his jacket.

Kate watched it drop to the floor in awful fascination, unable to move at all now as she saw what a mess her temper had got her into.

'Tonight, Kate my beautiful shrew, we'll give the piano and the pinball machines a miss—as you so rightly stated, the couch is the real games arena.' His eyes were dark, narrowed on her, and he smiled unpleasantly. Kate made a lunge to escape him, but he pushed her back, held her there with one hand while with the other, he unfastened the buttons of his shirt until it gaped almost to the waist.

He sat down beside her and hauled her across his knee. 'Now let me see.' His eyes ran over the rumpled black dress consideringly, lingering on the deep neckline where her skin paled. 'As I recall, you were wearing rather less, my dear.'

'No, no!' she cried, remembering the picture of herself half naked and holding her arms up for him.

'Yes, yes,' he insisted, his hands smoothing the black fabric from her shoulders as his mouth came down on hers to smother her protests. But the kiss had none of the gentleness of that night about it—it was bitter and punishing, and Kate tried to push this stranger away, longing for the man who had coerced and persuaded and—cared. It was a peculiar thing to think in the circumstances and enough to set free the tears that had hovered precariously all night, since she had seen him with Sonia again.

Robert straightened and looked down at her—her shoulders and the upper curves of her breasts bared, her hair tossed and stranded beech-copper against her skin. All the fight had gone from her and she stared up at him, tears magnifying the green of her eyes, and slipping down the slopes of her cheekbones. Robert closed his eyes for a moment, then flipped her dress into place and sat her up.

'It isn't you who's the victim, Kate,' he said in a voice suddenly weary, and left her sitting there alone while he paced about, his hands deep in his pockets and his gaze frowningly on the floor. She could have gone then and he wouldn't have stopped her, but something kept her there—waiting.

'When I first saw you, Kate,' he said harshly, 'I thought—this is a girl I want to know, this is a girl I want—a feminine, spirited girl, open and honest enough to admit what was there between us immediately.'

Her heart began a heavy knocking at her ribs.

'Then I discovered who you were and wished I'd never sent an accusing letter about a damned sign—and wished to hell I'd never written to the newspaper. And I wanted to find a way around it—so that the beautiful girl I'd just met would continue to look at me with that dazed look in her green eyes. Instead she turned into a nasty little bitch—hard and sharp-tongued in the face of my efforts to backtrack. I thought I'd been mistaken.'

It was true—Kate remembered his reluctance to produce Philip's picture. She had stubbornly refused to accept his olive branch.

Robert looked at her as if she might have something to say. But she remained silent, wondering at the strained look of him and where this might lead.

'So I treated her accordingly and saw her drive away from me with tears in her eyes, which made me think I was mistaken again.' He threw back his head and stared at the raked ceiling, the lines of his body squared with tension. 'The cycle sounds familiar, doesn't it, Kate? So—I offered an apology to this soft, feminine creature who cried because I·had been so harsh and what did I find? She turned into a virago again. This girl hates me, I thought, but couldn't quite put out of my mind the look on her face the first time I saw her. So I decided to stick around—make excuses to see her . . . Does all this bore you, Kate?' He turned on her suddenly and almost snarled the words. 'Because I'm finding it a bit tedious myself. I'm not accustomed to going around in circles.'

Kate put up a shaking hand to push back her hair and looked away from his steady gaze.

'I'm sorry I was so—rough with you just now,' he said in a tight voice. 'You make me so mad . . . Just answer me one question, honestly, Kate. Then I'll take you back to your guests and never bother you again.'

This time Kate couldn't stem the hope that filled her.

There was bitterness in his tone as if she'd hurt him, and surely she couldn't have done that unless his feelings were involved. 'Rob has a few vulnerable spots,' Dave had told her. Dyan had found them, but was it possible that she herself had?

'Do you dislike me too much, Kate? Is there any point in trying to sort it all out?'

She stared at him. This could be ended quite simply. All she had to say—flippantly, as was her style, was, 'That's two questions and I'm all out of answers,' and he would give up. She hesitated, gazing desperately at one of his pictures and thinking of Sonia bestowing her smile on another man down in the gallery—of the painter who had once turned Robert down. Her eyes flew back to him in sudden recollection. Now she knew why the wall in the living room had looked empty! The painting of mother and child had gone.

'No. Yes,' she said huskily, and he let out an exasperated breath.

'You just can't be honest, can you, Kate? No—yes. What kind of an answer is that?' His voice was hard, flat and he lowered his head in defeat.

'You asked me two questions, Robert. I gave you two answers.'

His chin came up at that and moments passed as he recalled his words. A new light gleamed in his eyes. 'In that case,' he said as he came towards her, 'let's sort it out.' He pulled her from the couch and into his arms. 'I could cheerfully kill you, Kate.' The muscle along his jaw tightened. 'But first . . .' His kiss was scarcely better than the last one, but this time Kate recognised the tension and the frustration that moved his lips so rigidly on hers. She struggled to get her arms free, but Robert raised his head and crushed her closer.

'Already regretting it, Kate? I should have known you

couldn't make even a small commitment. Do you want to be free?'

She nodded and bleakly he let her go.

'Just my arms,' she said, and slid them about his neck, 'so that I can hold you too.'

For a moment he stared as if not quite trusting, then gathered her close.

'Kate!' The sound was thick and muffled as he buried his face in her hair. She felt the release of tension in him, felt the knotted muscles of his shoulders relax under her fingers and revelled in her power to make it so. So she held him and knew that he needed her touch as much as she needed his. It was like coming home, and she was staggered that she had ever fought against it. She tilted her face for his kiss and her lips moved willingly with his. The need for pretence had gone and she responded with all the passion that had been waiting so long for release.

Robert drew back, his breathing uneven, his grey eyes intense. Wordlessly he studied her, then put up a hand to touch her hair and the gesture was unbelievably gentle.

'The night you were here, Kate, I wanted you so badly and you seemed to have warmed to me at last. It was tempting to keep you with me, but I knew I'd given you too much to drink—hoping to get under your guard I suppose——' his mouth twisted wryly. 'I had visions of you hating me again the next day.' He lifted a handful of fiery hair and watched it slip silken through his fingers. 'We'd moved so fast from fighting to liking and I—thought it might spoil everything if I rushed you into love. The hazards of a short cut seemed too great.' His eyes dropped to her face again. 'You were so damned defensive that I knew I couldn't tell you the reason I'd stopped was to protect you from yourself. But I didn't bargain on your interpretation of my very heroic,' his hand twisted in her hair and she winced, 'abstinence. I've never felt more helpless in my life.'

'I'm sorry. It wasn't for a while later that I questioned that. Then it occurred to me that I'd noticed certain—signs that you might not have wanted to stop and I wondered . . .'

'Why the hell didn't you let me explain the next day?' he demanded. 'I wasn't quite certain just how I would do so without rousing your temper, but I was hoping to find a way. But you didn't even give me a chance. All that rubbish about not remembering . . .' he grinned suddenly and mocked her words—' "you stopped! Oh, I wondered about that"—that's when I knew it was all an act.'

Kate bit her lip. 'So was the phone conversation with Andrew.'

'Do you mean you led the poor guy on like that just to give me the wrong idea?'

'No. It wasn't Andrew at all. Some man just happened to phone asking about pottery wine jugs and I. . .'

Robert's mouth dropped open. Then he threw back his head and roared. 'My God, Kate—the poor devil! He must have thought he was going crazy!'

'No, he thought I was unhinged.'

'So all that business about going away with Barrett was so much flak you shot at me?'

'He did ask me to go with him. But I'd decided not to long before I—we—you,' he chuckled over her stammering, 'before I came here,' she finished up, and glanced at the painting of the nude over the bar.

'And you jumped to conclusions when you saw me putting an overnight bag in the van later. Actually I was going to deliver some jars to a Lodge up near the Scenic Rim.'

'Why didn't you say so, then?' there was exasperation

in his voice, though he held her tenderly, his hands moving in a ceaseless caress on her back.

'My rotten temper, I suppose. If it's any consolation I spent the day in the rain forest wondering if you were jealous and thinking about you constantly. And I made up my mind to see you and find out why you didn't—press your advantage in the games room.'

His lips quirked. 'What a quaint turn of phrase you have, sweetheart!'

She ploughed on doggedly. 'And when I did—Sonia Marsden was here.'

'Ah, Sonia.' Robert took a deep breath. 'Yes, she did rather make her entrance at the wrong moment. Sonia is rather apt to do that.'

'She said——' Kate stopped. 'I got the impression that you and she were—close.'

'I wasn't above letting you think that. There were times when I wanted any response at all from you, Kate, and those occasional flashes of jealousy about Sonia were heartening. But the day she walked in on us here wasn't what you might have thought. She hadn't been here all night. She's never been here all night. Her father is a valued client and I took her out a few times—she called in to the gallery with or without her friends. Our relationship was going nowhere and she knew it—but Sonia likes to have a man to show off, and she clung to me until she found someone else. And it suited me to let her.'

Kate thought of the man with his arm about the girl's waist earlier. 'Was that her new boy-friend with her tonight?'

'Yes.' He brushed his lips on hers, teased a little with his tongue and drew back satisfied with her gasp of pleasure. 'I came alone to your show tonight, Kate, hoping to find a way through to you.'

'But you were so angry—about the Ransome business.'

He pressed her close and gave a snort of laughter 'The mysterious B. Ransome!' He became serious for a moment. 'You have talent, Kate. Are you ambitious?'

His past love Dyan had been ambitious. Kate felt a surge of envy that she had been his love and gratitude that she had turned him down.

'Very,' she assured him. 'I want to be awarded first prize by that well-known critic, Robert Beaumont. Not,' she hastened to add, 'necessarily for painting.'

His smile held a vestige of relief and Kate knew she had made the right answer. 'You win my first prize right now for being the most maddening, provoking woman I've ever met,' he told her in a tender-rough tone. 'I hope you won't always be so obstreperous?' In mock trepidation he eyed her fiery hair and Kate shook her head, trying to find the words to explain her resistance. Absently, she put a hand to the gold chain at his neck to touch the cold metal, then moved on to lightly explore the warm contours of his chest, bared by his open shirt.

'I was afraid, Robert. When I saw you at the studio—I'd never felt like that before. I never intended to let anyone have the power over me that my mother had over my father. So I suppose I backed off and convinced myself that you were all the things I detested. But you kept whittling away at my image of you and in the end . . .'

In her ear he whispered, 'Yes—in the end——?' He pressed his mouth to her neck, marking a trail of kisses to her temple and Kate closed her eyes.

'In the end—there's just one thing I want explained,' she announced unsteadily. 'Why did you write to us so rudely about the sign?'

He gave a muffled groan. 'The blasted sign! God, how I've regretted that. I came back from abroad and was snowed under with work. Ben Strickland came to

…e about the sign and told me a few things about your
…lace that made me think it was like another one that
…t up in Lindale a while back—a cheap, quick-profit
…lace selling mass-produced imports and prints dressed
…p to look like originals. It went out of business very
…st. And I hate to say it, but the day I went in and
…ought Philip's picture I really didn't look closely
…nough to see that your place wasn't that kind.'

'But why would Ben Strickland say things about us?
…e hasn't even spoken to us!'

'It seemed Ben had been trying to scrape up the
…oney to buy your cottage and land. I think he'd been
…lanning on starting a business of his own for a long
…me. The house had stood empty for so long that I
…ink he imagined he only had to find the money to
…alise his dream. Then two women appeared out of the
…ue and snatched it from under his nose. Worse—
…ey made it into the kind of place he wanted himself.'

'We had no idea . . .' Kate thought of the weighty,
…alding man she'd only seen twice—at the C.A.G. Show
…d in town. He had avoided her eyes on both
…casions, and now she knew why.

'Neither did I until lately. He drafted the letter about
…e sign and I'm afraid I was just busy enough to sign it
…ithout questioning that it might be unwarranted.'

Kate choked back a giggle at her own accuracy. That
…st letter was the one that had cemented the pasty,
…erfed image of the writer in her mind. And she'd been
…ght. Except that the writer hadn't been Robert at all
…t Ben Strickland.

'And my letter to the papers wasn't totally aimed at
…u but inspired by my contempt for the other so-called
…llery and Ben's talk about more unethical newcomers.
…here was no reason to doubt him—but of course, I
…ould have checked. I've kicked myself since for not
…ing so.'

'What would have happened, I wonder, if you'd ju
dropped in one day and introduced yourself?' Ka
smiled.

'The same thing would have happened, but a l
faster. You've made me work damned hard to win yo
Kate.' Robert gripped a handful of her hair and tipp
her head back. 'You've tried my temper and trampl
on my ego and turned me inside out wondering what
could do next to keep myself in the picture with you.

'Staying "in the picture" would hardly be a proble
for a man of art like yourself,' she grinned.

'It isn't usually,' he admitted modestly, 'but y
forced me to new inventiveness.'

'The jogging?' Kate raised her eyebrows, 'was th
one of your ploys to keep dropping by?'

'Yes. I run every day anyway, but usually on my ow
land and never on a steep grade. Still, the downhill t
wasn't too bad. Uphill was a bit of a strain for m
being an "older man",' he reminded her of her gib
and she laughed.

'I was very impressed, you know, especially when yo
said you ran all the way back again. A mile uphill eve
day! That was going to extremes just to see me.' Ka
looked a little smug at the extent of his sacrifice.

'Mmm.' Robert was sheepish. 'Of course, it wasn
always a mile back.'

She pulled away to inspect him. 'What do you—
she thought of his figure that day on the road, tall a
broad-shouldered in the tracksuit, reflected in her si
mirror as she'd passed him in the van. Her memo
tripped—she had passed a car—a parked car, only
white blur at the time.

'You cheated!' she exclaimed. 'You drove half t
way and parked your car there!'

'A little cheating seemed called for. Anyway, ev
half the distance is worthy of applause,' he proteste

And I'd already done a circuit of my own place before
set out each day to ensnare a copper-headed witch.
For a while I thought all I would get out of it was the
exercise.'

Kate laughed with him. It seemed crazy that she had
been so afraid of turning out a loser like her father that
she had almost missed this man entirely. Now she was
warmly certain that the balance of power was equal.
Robert was as vulnerable as she, and the thought was
humbling. Her hands roamed his chest, slipping under
his shirt to slide up to his shoulders and then around
the breadth of him. It was a belated exploration—a
giving way to the restraint that had kept her so long
from touching him. In a kind of wonder she raised
herself on tiptoe and put her mouth to his, brazenly
taking the initiative to kiss him, knowing there were no
barriers left.

'My God, Kate,' he breathed when they pulled apart,
'When you give, you give everything, don't you?'

'Only to you,' she said simply, and was swept away
in his answer. She hadn't realised that love could be
told so eloquently by a lingering kiss, by the caring,
tender language of touch.

His whispered words were mere confirmation. 'I love
you, Kate.'

'You've already told me,' she said. 'I love you too.'

'Shall we say it again?'

'Yes, please—and again . . .' and they spoke to each
other with no words at all.

Robert picked her up and the raked, raftered ceiling
circled by in a replay of that other night. But this time
he wouldn't leave her alone on the red velvet couch,
Kate thought exultantly, and clasped her arms about
his neck, her answer already forming as he spoke.

'Marry me, Kate?' and her, 'Yes,' fitted in without a
second between the question.

He lowered her to the settee and watched her for moment.

'Just one more thing, B. Ransome. What does the "F stand for?'

'Guess.' Kate put up a hand and took his.

'Belinda——?' he said as she drew him down to he 'Beryl? Blanche——?'

Kate's arms went about him. 'Besotted,' she said, an against her mouth Robert guessed again.

'Beloved.'

Coming Next Month in Harlequin Romances!

2665 PETER'S SISTER Jeanne Allan
A battle-scarred Vietnam veteran shows up in Colorado and triggers painful memories in his buddy's sister. He reminds her of the brother she lost and the love she's never forgotten.

2666 ONCE FOR ALL TIME Betty Neels
When tragedy strikes a London nurse, support comes — not from her fiancé — but from her supervising doctor. But she finds little comfort, knowing he's already involved with another woman.

2667 DARKER FIRE Morgan Patterson
Because she so desperately needs the job, a Denver secretary lies about her marital status. But how can she disguise her feelings when her boss asks her to leave her husband and marry him instead?

2668 CHÂTEAU VILLON Emily Spenser
Her wealthy French grandfather tries to make amends for having disinherited her father. Instead, he alienates Camille and the winery's heir when he forces them to marry before love has a chance to take root.

2669 TORMENTED RHAPSODY Nicola West
The idea of returning to the tiny Scottish village of her childhood tantalizes and torments a young Englishwoman. Inevitably, she'll run into the man who once broke her heart with his indifference.

2670 CATCH A FALLING STAR Rena Young
Everyone in the music business calls her the Ice Maiden. But there's one man in Australia capable of melting her reserve — if only to sign her with his nearly bankrupt recording company.

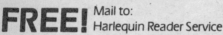